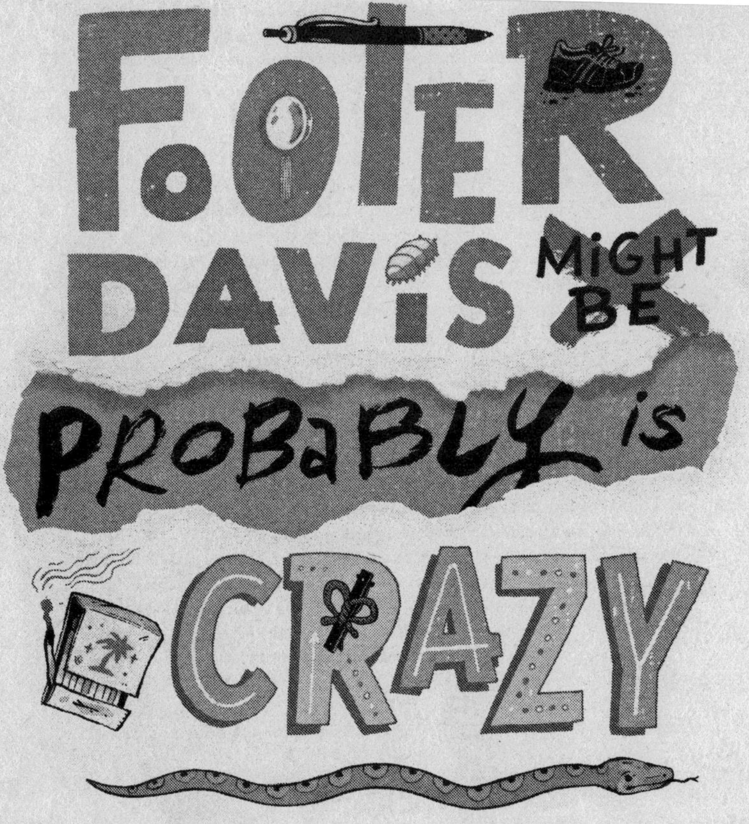

Susan Vaught

A Paula Wiseman Book
Simon & Schuster Books for Young Readers
New York • London • Toronto • Sydney • New Delhi

SIMON & SCHUSTER BOOKS FOR YOUNG READERS
An imprint of Simon & Schuster Children's Publishing Division
1230 Avenue of the Americas, New York, New York 10020

For information about special discounts for bulk purchases, please contact Simon & Schuster Special Sales at 1-866-506-1949 or business@simonandschuster.com.
The Simon & Schuster Speakers Bureau can bring authors to your live event. For more information or to book an event, contact the Simon & Schuster Speakers Bureau at 1-866-248-3049 or visit our website at www.simonspeakers.com.
Also available in a Simon & Schuster Books for Young Readers hardcover edition
Book design by Laurent Linn
The text for this book is set in Minister Std.
Manufactured in the United States of America
0817 OFF
First Simon & Schuster Books for Young Readers paperback edition March 2016
4 6 8 10 9 7 5 3
The Library of Congress has cataloged the hardcover edition as follows:
Vaught, Susan, 1955–
Footer Davis probably is crazy / Susan Vaught.
pages cm
"A Paula Wiseman Book."
Summary: Ten-year-old Footer and her friends investigate when a nearby farm is burned, the farmer murdered, and his children disappear, but as they follow the clues, Footer starts having flashbacks and wonders if she is going crazy like her mother, who is back in a mental institution near their Mississippi home.
ISBN 978-1-4814-2276-5 (hc)
[1. Mental illness—Fiction. 2. Arson—Fiction. 3. Missing children—Fiction. 4. Family life—Mississippi—Fiction. 5. Friendship—Fiction. 6. Mississippi—Fiction. 7. Mystery and detective stories.] I. Reinhardt, Jennifer Black, 1963– illustrator. II. Title.
PZ7.V4673Foo 2015
[Fic]—dc23
2014009437
ISBN 978-1-4814-2277-2 (pbk)
ISBN 978-1-4814-2278-9 (eBook)

For Holly and Missy, two of my cousin-sisters,
because you know how much of this is true.
I love you both very much.

CHAPTER 1

Nine Days After the Fire

The day my mother exploded a copperhead snake with an elephant gun, I decided I was genetically destined to become a felon or a big-game hunter. That was good, since I had tried being a ballerina, poet, artist, and musician, and I sucked at all of those.

Mom cleaned out a third of the water from our backyard pond with the snake shot, but that wasn't the best part. "You flew backward up the hill seven whole feet." I prodded her hip with my toe. "That was special. You should try out for the circus."

The air smelled like spring flowers and gunpowder. Mom grunted and said something like "crouton," and something else that sounded like a swear word. She was probably trying to tell me to burn the snake's carcass, because that's what she did with all the snakes she killed.

"We don't have to burn the snake," I told her. "Nothing left of this one."

Mom's red hair splayed across the pine needles under her head, and her pretzel-shaped barrettes glittered in the sunlight. I couldn't stand those barrettes. They looked like something little kids wore. A bruise was spreading across Mom's shoulder and chest. The elephant gun lay in the holly bushes across the yard. Wicked. I couldn't believe it flew that far. My BB gun, Louise, punched like a scared little sister when I fired her. Dad's big rifle had to kick like a rhinoceros.

I was carrying Louise because Peavine and his sister, Angel, were on their way over so we could go searching for two kids who went missing after a fire, but I figured I should keep Louise out of Mom's line of sight. I set her down behind me, careful to keep my hand on her barrel so I didn't drop her in the grass. After that kickback, one look at a BB gun might send Mom straight into a screaming fit.

Mom had on green eye shadow that matched her shirt and sandals and her brand-new bruise. The sandals had green sparklies, too, the same color as her eyes, which I couldn't see because she kept squeezing them shut. "Dad's gonna be ticked that you pried open his gun case," I said.

"Crouton," Mom mumbled. And then I realized she was trying to say, "Call your father," except she couldn't open her mouth all the way.

"It's okay," I told her. "I hear sirens. They might be after you, but Captain Armstrong's charging up and down the main road in his running clothes and hollering 'INCOMING,' so maybe it's him they want."

"Fontana. Call. Your father."

"Fiiiine." She just *had* to use my proper name. *Blech.* I pulled my phone out of my pocket and speed-dialed Dad while I asked her, "Aren't you glad he won the fight about getting me a phone?"

Mom didn't answer.

The phone rang twice before Dad picked up with, "Honey, you know I'm busy."

I could hear people talking in the background because he worked as a dispatch officer in Bugtussle, Mississippi's 9-1-1 call center. It was an important job, and a good one to have, with Mom as his wife and me as his daughter.

"Mom shot a copperhead with your old Nitro Express rifle," I told him. "We'll be picking snake guts off the roof for a year."

It got so quiet on Dad's end that I could almost make out what the other operators were saying. A lot of those calls were probably about the blast that just came from Sixty Erlanger Lane, because canon fire was unusual in our neighborhood. We lived on a nice cul-de-sac, in a big house with a basement that backed up to a pond in front of some woods. In Mississippi, all water had snakes, especially if it was muddy. Snakes didn't care what kind of neighborhood you lived in.

Mom groaned and shifted on the ground. A piece of mangled copperhead blopped off a nearby pine branch, which would have grossed me out if I had been a normal girl, but I was so far from normal, it wasn't even funny—except, of course, when it was.

"I'll be right home," Dad said. I waited for it, and a second later it came. "I'm sorry, Footer. I know this has got to stop."

The History of Bugtussle, Mississippi

Footer Davis
5th Period
Ms. Perry

1. The Meaning of "Bugtussle"

Bugtussle, Mississippi, got a name with "bug" in it because it has way too many doodlebugs.

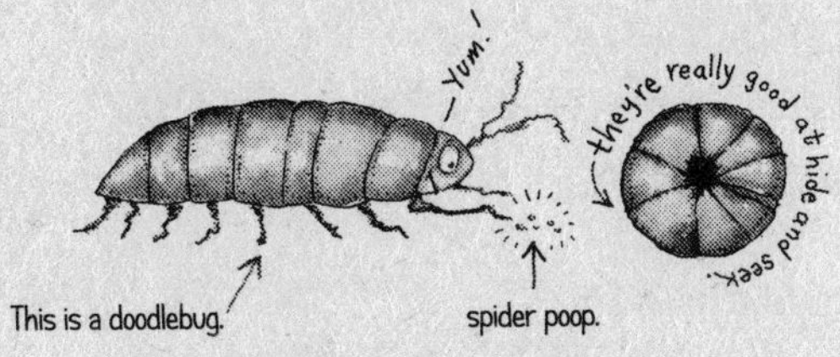

Yum!
they're really good at hide and seek.
This is a doodlebug.
spider poop.

C–
More text, less illustration. Spider poop is not relevant to the town's founding. Please take your assignments more seriously.

Kingdom: Animalia
Phylum: Arthropoda
Subphylum: Crustacea ← like crabs and lobsters and shrimp
Class: Malacostraca
Order: Isopoda
Suborder: Oniscidea
Family: Armadillidiidae
Genera: Armadillidium
Species: vulgare

Doodlebugs are a type of wood louse. They are also called pill bugs, and roly-polies. When they get upset, they roll into balls. Lizards like to eat them, but then the lizards get poisoned. Doodlebugs must be good at revenge. Some people who keep spiders for pets also keep doodlebugs, to eat spider poop and mold.

II. What I Learned from This Report

1. Spiders poop.
2. My town is named after a wood louse.
3. Whoever named our town was probably weird, because only a weirdo names a town after lice.

CHAPTER 2

Nine Days After the Fire—Maybe Almost Nine and One-Half Days

Ambulance driver: Your shoulder may be broken, Ms. Davis. I'd like you to come with me.

Mom: My shoulder is fine, and no. I don't like ambulances and hospitals.

Captain Armstrong: Adele, they don't mean you any harm. I know it's hard, but let them look.

Dad: Please, honey. Let's just get your arm checked.

Mom: I said it's fine. I didn't mean to pick the wrong gun, but snakes need to die. Besides, Peavine and Angel came over to play.

Captain Armstrong: I'll watch the kids.

Mom: No.

Ambulance driver: I'll do whatever you want, Mr. Davis.

Dad: Footer, why don't you and your friends head on over to wherever you're going? Just be back before dark.

When life gets too weird, my brain cuts everything down to freeze-frames. *Click.* Dad was there. *Click.* Captain Armstrong was there. *Click.* The ambulance pulled up. *Click.* All the neighbors came out to stare. I so didn't want to stay around and get gawked at. So, Peavine, Angel, and I headed for the woods. They didn't say anything about the neighbors and ambulance circus. They were too used to it, like me.

Everybody in Bugtussle knew about my mother.

Adele Davis, she's a pretty thing, but she ain't right, bless her heart.

That's what people said behind my back, and to my face. People who don't live in Mississippi think "bless your heart" means something nice, but it really means they think you're too stupid to bother trying to explain things to you, or that you're too crazy to help. People never say what they mean, except for Peavine, which is why he's my best friend, and why I'd rather think about him than my mom, whether her heart got blessed or not.

Sometimes I'd rather think about anything other than my mom, like how Peavine and Angel were going to help me search what was left of the Abrams farm. Everybody else in Bugtussle knew about the murder and fire at the Abrams farm too, even if nobody could figure out how they happened, or why.

Cissy Abrams was twelve, one year older than me. Doc was only six. I knew them a little bit, from seeing them around town and going to the farm a few times with Mom to take over some fudge at Christmas and stuff. She visited over there a lot, but she didn't usually take me, because, she said, *Sweetie, they have a few problems, and Mr. Abrams just needs a little help.*

Cissy and Doc's dad, Carl Abrams, got locked in prison for selling drugs, and their mom lived down in Jackson. She didn't have custody of Cissy and Doc, because she used meth and didn't have any teeth and couldn't take care of kids in her condition. Since old Ms. Abrams died from cancer, old Mr. Abrams raised Cissy and Doc by himself on his farm, which backed up to Wynwood Heights, where I lived. He believed in homeschooling, and he mostly kept to himself and made Cissy and Doc stay home and tend to farm chores and lessons. They weren't allowed to have fun, not really, and I felt pretty bad for them.

Then, just after the first of April, nine days ago, somebody shot Mr. Abrams to death and burned the whole place to the ground.

I didn't remember much about that Friday night, except

waking up to the stench of smoke and a bunch of screaming sirens, and realizing Mom and Dad weren't in the house. I'd been about to go out looking for them when Mom came upstairs. She looked exhausted. When Dad got back from his night shift, he was all frowns and head shaking.

It's bad, he told us. I had a thousand questions, but Mom just nodded and I knew better than to ask anything. Mom couldn't handle too much stress, and I didn't want to make her cry and have bad dreams and start talking about things that weren't real.

Later, the police said it was arson and that Cissy and Doc died in the fire. Then the Mississippi Bureau of Investigation said maybe Cissy and Doc didn't die, because nobody found any pieces of them, not even teeth, and teeth weren't supposed to burn.

It was a mystery.

"The Nitro Express." Peavine poled along on his arm crutches and whistled. "I've always wanted to shoot that thing."

"Firearms are dangerous," Angel said, following behind him through the woods, reading her book as she walked the packed-dirt path. "They should be outlawed."

I squeezed Louise's stock and pressed her hard against the strap of my backpack. "Second amendment says we can have guns," I told her. "Don't you listen in social studies? Do they even have social studies in third grade? I can't remember."

Angel, who really did look like an angel, with her golden curls and blue eyes and the bright, ruffly dresses she wore, kept reading her science-fiction book. The stupid thing was thicker than two bricks. Angel was only eight, but she had a thirty-year-old brain, and she talked like a politician. That's why she had no friends and she had to hang out with us. Peavine and I, we looked after Angel, because our parents expected us to, and because she grows on you after a while, kind of like a nasty toenail fungus.

"A well regulated militia, being necessary to the security of a free state, the right of the people to keep and bear arms, shall not be infringed," she said. "I don't think school shootings and your mom obliterating helpless snakes count as the actions of a well-regulated militia."

"Leave off," Peavine warned, and Angel went back to her book.

"It's okay," I told him, because arguing about guns and the Constitution was better than worrying about Mom and whether or not she would go to the hospital. It was better than thinking about Captain Armstrong and the clump of other neighbors standing in front of the four other houses on our cul-de-sac gaping at Mom while she tugged her shiny new barrettes back into place and argued with Dad and the ambulance driver.

Would Dad go with Mom? Would he call Peavine and Angel's mom to come to the house to look after us? Ms.

Jones always helped out. She could do that because she didn't have problems like Mom did.

My eyes darted to Peavine and then to Angel.

Must be nice, having a real *mom.*

Wow, that was mean. And I didn't believe that. Not really. My mom was a real mom, and a good one. She just got different sometimes.

I don't think school shootings and your mom obliterating helpless snakes count as the actions of a well-regulated militia. . . .

My face burned at the edges, even though pine trees shaded us as we walked. "Pit vipers aren't helpless, Angel," I said. "If a copperhead bites you, you get sick and puke, and your foot can fall off."

"Yeah." Peavine's short blond hair looked almost white in the sunlight filtering through the branches. With every swing of his legs he tipped like he would fall, but he never did. He was graceful, like a dancer or an acrobat, and he filled out his black T-shirt with more muscles than most boys I knew. I was the one who always got my feet tangled and cut my knees.

"Is your mother off her medication again?" Angel asked, still reading as she walked.

I glared at the back of her head. "Not that I know of. She doesn't always tell us."

Actually, she *never* told us. Sometimes Mom flushed her pills down the toilet or threw them away. Not long ago, she hid a bunch in the backyard under some bushes near the pond. I found them when I was burying a squirrel the neighbor's cat killed on our doorstep. Mom was upset about that squirrel, because she fed it peanut butter and toast every morning. The medicine probably would have helped her not cry so much when it died.

"You remembered the camera, right?" Peavine asked, probably because he knew I didn't want to talk about Mom. I never wanted to talk about Mom. What could I say, anyway?

Yeah, she's nuts.

Yeah, it sucks.

Yeah, one day I might be crazier than she is.

Bleh.

"My new phone's camera is fine," I told Peavine. "And your notebook is in the backpack, with the magnifying glass. We're set."

"I read the clippings again," Angel said. "Nobody had a motive to murder Mr. Abrams and take Cissy and Doc. It had to be some kind of accident."

"Mr. Abrams got shot dead," Peavine called over his shoulder. "How could that be an accident? And the fire was set on purpose. Police said so."

"People get shot by mistake," Angel said. "Fires can be set by accident too."

I didn't argue with her, because once I tried an experiment with a magnifying glass and a bunch of newspapers, only I used too many newspapers and the grass was really dry and the sun was bright. At least the fire department didn't charge for the visit. The fence didn't catch fire with the newspapers, and I only messed up one corner of the yard, but it took me three months of allowance and chores to pay Dad back for the dirt and sod.

Did Cissy Abrams use a magnifying glass inside her house? Was it possible to set a whole house on fire with a magnifying glass? But even if she made a mistake like I did, how did the barn burn, and who shot her grandfather?

"Makes no sense." Angel finally closed her book because we were getting to the end of the half-mile trail from my backyard to the edge of the Abrams farm. "Cissy and Doc probably died in the fire."

"I think somebody stole them," Peavine said. Each time he planted his poles in the dry ground, puffs of dust scattered across his jeans, then drifted into the leaves and branches beside the path.

I couldn't smell the dust. My nose was still full of gunpowder, but I knew that scent wasn't exactly real, because of another science experiment that used coffee and didn't involve any fire departments. We learned in class that smell works by molecules, so noses can literally fill up with smells, and you can keep smelling them even if you're not around them anymore. We sniffed coffee for a while. Then the teacher took it away, and we could still smell it for a few minutes.

I wondered if Mom could still smell the gunpowder from where she shot the snake. Did she get in the ambulance? Was her shoulder really busted? Would they make her stay overnight, or maybe take her up to Memphis again, like last summer? I hated it when Mom had to be gone a long time.

"Okay," Peavine said, swinging to a halt as the woods ended.

Angel stopped beside him, and I pulled up next to her. Across the field full of ryegrass nobody was alive to mow, burned timbers of the house and barn jutted up like black skeletons. Broken tape slithered at the corners whenever the breeze picked up. It had been bright yellow when we first saw it, and stretched tight around the crime scene. Guys in uniforms and funny suits combed over the place for hours and days while Peavine and Angel and I watched from right about where we stood now. Local police, the Mississippi Bureau of Investigation, the Federal Bureau of Investigation—everybody came and looked.

They didn't find anything except what was left of Mr. Abrams after somebody blew him away with a shotgun, but they kept a guard on the place until yesterday. The police no longer considered the Abrams case an "active investigation," so we figured we'd finally get our chance to take a closer look.

It's not safe, Fontana, Mom's voice whispered in my head. *There might be snakes in those ashes.*

Mom thought snakes were everywhere. Snakes didn't much bother me, but now that we were at the Abrams farm, I wondered if snakes might be better than what really lay beneath the ashes. The stench of char chased away the gunpowder lodged in my nose. My stomach felt funny.

Angel coughed. "I used to like that smell. Now it makes me think of dead people."

"There aren't any dead people," Peavine said. "The police took the body away."

He started forward and I went with him, but Angel hung back. "It's not like they could sweep up all the people ashes," she called after us. "Mr. Abrams is still right here—or some of him is! And maybe Cissy and Doc, too."

I couldn't see Peavine's face, but I figured he was rolling his eyes.

Sometimes Angel made too much sense. I hated that, but no way was I giving up a chance to touch a crime scene. Peavine wanted to be a detective one day. Since big-game hunter and felon weren't immediate options for me, I was currently thinking about taking up journalism because all artistic pursuits seemed to be out of the question, and because detectives and journalists worked together all the time. At least, on TV they did. We had already interviewed Mom about the fire, and we had plans to talk to suspects like Dad and my neighbor Captain

Armstrong, and look around for suspicious strangers too. In a crime that didn't make any sense, everybody had to be a suspect, right? I would ask the questions, and Peavine would write down the answers, since he scribbled faster than me, and detectives were always supposed to be taking notes on suspect behavior and . . . *demeanor*. That was the word.

My nerves jumped and danced like the police tape. I didn't know Cissy or Doc or Mr. Abrams as well as Mom did, so I shouldn't have been too icked out about touching their ashes.

From somewhere far off behind us, a siren wailed. The sound crawled up and down my skin like one of Bugtussle's roly-polies, and I had to rub my arms to make it stop. Mom. Either Dad and Captain Armstrong and the ambulance driver got her to go to the hospital, or they called for help and took her against her will.

I walked a little faster, getting ahead of Peavine. Skeletons and dead-people ashes were easier than Mom. There was nothing I could do about Mom, *bless her heart*. I probably couldn't do much about Cissy and Doc being disappeared either, but it didn't hurt to try at least.

From the Notebook of Detective Peavine Jones

Interview of Adele Davis, Eight Days After the Fire

Location: Television Room in Footer's House

Footer: Peavine and I want to ask you some questions about the Abrams fire, Mom. [Journalist has a pretty smile.]

Ms. Davis: I need to remember peanut butter. We're almost out, and I have to get some at the store. Peanut butter, jelly, and bread, too. I can't forget.

Footer: Mom, can we talk about the fire? Please?

Ms. Davis: Peavine, don't you think Fontana is beautiful? Her eyes are so bright and green. Write that down. [Suspect puts her fingertips under Journalist's eye, making Journalist do her eating-lemons look.] Don't you want to dress a little better, honey? Something other than those old jeans and that

T-shirt. I could get you a haircut. Wouldn't a haircut be good?

Footer: [Journalist pulls away from suspect, scrubs her face with her palm.] Mom. The fire. Can you tell us what you remember about the night of the fire?

Ms. Davis: I know, I know. You like your nickname better. Footer. I tell everybody how Peavine came up with that when you were both three, and he couldn't talk plainly yet because of his cerebral palsy, so "Footer" was as close as he could get to your actual name. You're a good kid, Peavine, but I don't want Footer to marry you.

Footer: Mom!

Ms. Davis: [Suspect pats my head.] You're a good kid. You remind me of Fontana's father at that age. I just don't want Fontana to marry you because she should go to college and get a job, then use her degree somewhere far away from here—maybe even to be a real journalist, instead of all this play-around stuff. She can do better than Bugtussle. I don't want her to be tied to this town.

Footer: Peavine, let's interview Dad instead.

Me: Why don't you want Footer to stay in Bugtussle, suspect? I mean Ms. Davis?

Ms. Davis: There are too many snakes in Bugtussle. Have you seen them, Peavine? [Suspect looks anxious.]

Me: I—

Ms. Davis: If you find a snake, you should shoot it and burn the pieces. That's the only way to be sure snakes are gone forever.

Footer: Mom, what does that mean?

Ms. Davis: Just what I said, sweetie. Just exactly what I said. [Suspect walks away from us, toward the kitchen.]

CHAPTER 3

Still Nine and One-Half Days After the Fire

"*Dateline* figures it was a serial killer," I said. We'd been at the crime scene for about two hours. Squinting through the sweat on my safety glasses, I shot at a dirt clod Peavine had balanced on a fence post outside what was left of the Abrams barn.

The BB hit the dirt clod and knocked it off beside Angel, who was digging in the ashes and somehow managing not to get any of the mess on her pink sundress. She picked up my phone and moved farther away, toward the house. The ashes of the house and barn met in the middle of a short walkway, smeared and mingled by fire hoses and wind. I wished we had some wind instead of the weak breeze. It was turning off hot, and there wasn't a cloud anywhere.

Peavine chose another clod, put it on the post, and

came to take his turn. "I saw that *Dateline* episode too. The guy said the killer probably murdered Mr. Abrams so he could steal Cissy and Doc and maybe torture them or put them in a basement somewhere, and they might get found alive when they're grown."

"It wasn't a serial killer." Angel stopped digging long enough to snap pictures of the dirt, then the woods, then the charred barn boards.

I pulled off my sweaty safety glasses and handed them to Peavine. After he got them on, I passed Louise to him and watched the dirt clod. "How do you know it wasn't a serial killer? You aren't psychic."

"I read all your serial killer books and some other ones too." Angel shrugged as she put down the phone and went back to poking at a charred rock. Her hands weren't even dirty. How did she *do* that? "It doesn't fit any of the what-they-call-its, right?"

"Profiles. And I don't know." I sighed, because Angel was right again. "Probably not."

Peavine shot the dirt clod. It didn't fall off the post. "Why not?" he asked.

"Serial killers usually kill kids *or* grown-ups." I took Louise and the glasses back and wiped them on my shirt. Then I put the glasses on my face, pumped Louise's handle, aimed, and knocked the clod to the ground with one shot. "Not kids *and* grown-ups. They like keeping everything the same."

I liked keeping everything the same too. I hoped that didn't give me too much in common with serial killers. I already had enough to worry about.

Peavine took the glasses and Louise, and I turned toward Angel and the burned boards of the Abrams house. Heat shimmered in the air, blurring everything, and I thought I saw the old farmhouse just like it used to be before it burned.

I turned back to Peavine, feeling jumpier than ever. I had only been to this farm a few times. Why was I thinking about it like I knew it better? And why did it look gray, like it was dark outside? The Abrams house had been white with a green roof, not gray. Peavine seemed wavy and thin in the hot air.

Cissy Abrams had black hair, and she was taller than Peavine.

The smell of smoke got so strong, I could taste it. My nose, the back of my throat—it almost choked me. My eyes watered from it, and my ears started to buzz. Something was happening. The world around me was changing, and I couldn't stop it, and I had no idea why, and my heart started beating so hard, I couldn't even talk.

Peavine lowered Louise after missing his dirt clod, and it got dark all of a sudden, and flames burst out around us. I sucked a breath of scorching air as heat seared my cheeks. Smoke clogged my nose, and my heart raced. Peavine disappeared, and Angel vanished as she dug in the ashes with her hands. *The barn loomed beside me, burning.*

Everything was on fire.

My whole body shook. Where was Peavine? And Angel—

Cissy Abrams walked out of the flames. She came and stood in front of me, silvery and pale in the moonlight. My mouth came open, but I didn't make any noise. I just stood there shaking. This wasn't real. It couldn't be real.

The buzz in my ears turned into a roar, then popping, then that weird sort of deafness I got when I jumped into the deep end of a pool and went down too far, too fast.

Cissy looked at me with blank eyes. Dark flecks covered her face and clothes, like soot, but it wasn't soot. I wanted to scream.

Mom appeared beside Cissy. She was talking, but I couldn't hear her. Then she said something a little louder. It sounded like hurry.

Mom looked up and saw me.

I started to fall.

Right before I hit the ground, Peavine flashed into view in front of me, and he grabbed my arms, and it was daytime again, and all the noises and smells stopped, and we were standing in the ashes of the Abrams farm. Nothing was burning. Cissy was gone, and my mother was gone, and it was now again, but I was still shaking so hard that my teeth chattered.

Peavine's grip on my arms tightened, but it didn't hurt. His wide, worried eyes stared into mine as he pulled me closer to him. "You look as lost as last year's Easter egg."

Click. Click. Angel was taking pictures of me.

"Sorry," I muttered as I turned my face away from the camera, glad Peavine was so close to me. He felt like a wall between me and Angel and everything in the whole world.

My brain turned circles in my skull until my whole head hurt.

"Did you get too hot or something?" Peavine asked.

For a second I thought he was going to hug me, and I wanted him to, and then I didn't. "I—um, yeah." I pulled away from him and tried to smile, but I don't think I made it, because I had never seen anything that wasn't there before, and I still wanted to scream. Mom heard things and saw things and laughed at nothing when she got sick, and I wasn't like her.

Click.

"Stop it," I told Angel. All of a sudden, I felt like somebody was watching us. My eyes darted to the woods around the barn, to the trees covered with patches of soot and ash, their burned branches dry and crumbling from the fire.

Click. Click. Click.

Was that a shadow there, under the brush beside that big oak?

No. I needed to stop. I turned my back on the tree. Peavine was looking at me like I'd gone totally insane. Angel was taking pictures of the edge of the path, near the oak.

There wasn't anything there but brush and leaves and grass. I *knew* that, but . . .

I'm not crazy. I'm not my mother.

Angel snapped another picture.

"Cut it out," Peavine told her.

She glared at me and then dropped the phone on the grass beside her. It snapped another picture by itself as she turned her attention back to the pile of ashes. My crumpled brain thought she was moving in slow motion as she pushed a rock aside, then picked something up and dusted it off.

My shaking got worse.

She rubbed more dirt and ash off her find, then laid it beside her along with a partly melted set of dice, a scorched piece of a little kid's tennis shoe, and a warped piece of plastic she'd already found. It was a pretzel-shaped barrette, just like my mother always wore.

CHAPTER 4

Definitely at Least Nine and One-Half Days After the Fire

Proof I'm Probably Going Crazy Like Mom

I look like Mom, so I probably have more of her genes than Dad's.
I say stupid stuff when I don't want to.
I make a lot of people mad, and sometimes not on purpose.
I am willful. Just ask Peavine's mom and my teachers.
I saw things at the Abrams farm that weren't real.

Proof I'm Probably Not Going Crazy Like Mom

Just because you look like a sick person doesn't mean you'll get sick.
Angel says stupider things than me, lots of times.
Some people need to get mad. Maybe I'm helping them talk about their problems.
"Willful" is another word for "determined," and "determined" sounds a lot better.
Maybe the Abrams farm is haunted and I saw ghosts.

I snuggled into Dad in his recliner and tried not to think about the Crazy List lying on my desk in my bedroom, or Crazy Mom, a quadrillion miles away in Memphis, locked away in the hospital again. The *other* kind of hospital.

We had the lights off, and we were supposed to be *settling down for bed*. Dad was big on early bedtimes when he had to run the show. He pulled up my Superman blanket until it covered my shoulders, then flicked on the DVR and punched the local news. It droned in the background. I yawned and stretched.

"Careful, there." Dad kissed the top of my head. "This old chair won't hold us both forever."

I put my face in Dad's chest and burped applesauce and hamburgers. The applesauce was because it counted as fruits or vegetables, and Dad tried to keep us healthy, at least a little bit. Plus, if Mom got home from the hospital and found out we had eaten nothing but junk food while she was gone, she'd throw a total fit.

Dad smelled like pine needles and his blue cotton pajamas. That sort of made me relax and sort of didn't, and the news talked about rain or not rain, and I said, "I miss her already."

"I do too." Dad kept his eyes on the news when I glanced up at him. TV shadows played and flickered across his face, but I could tell he was frowning.

"Are you going to look sad the whole time she's gone

this time?" I poked his chin with my fingertip.

"I don't know." He crossed his eyes as he looked down at me. "Are you?"

"Probably."

"Okay, then. We'll look sad together."

He uncrossed his eyes and went back to paying attention to the news, which had moved on to sports, which was even more boring than bake sales and weather.

I sighed. "Good dads would try to cheer up their daughters and pretend everything was going to be perfect."

"Good dads tell the truth and face it with their daughters." He put his hand on my head and stroked my hair. That usually made me sleepy, but tonight it just made me sigh all over again.

"So, what's the truth about Mom?" I asked him.

A few seconds went by before he answered. "The truth about Adele is, she'll come back to us as soon as she's able. And the truth about us is, we'll be waiting."

I picked at the corner of my blanket and didn't say anything. That was what I had wanted to hear, so why didn't it make me feel any better?

"Are you and Peavine still investigating the Abrams fire, Footer?"

"Since we're talking about truth and everything, I guess I have to tell it, so yes, sir."

It was Dad's turn to sigh. I rose up and down as his

chest heaved, then heard the rumble of his voice through his chest as he said, "You know I don't want you to do that. I don't think you should spend your energy on sad, terrible things."

"It keeps my mind off other sad, terrible things."

I went up and down again as Dad took a really deep breath. He rubbed my hair some more as he said, "Okay. But if I tell you to stop, I'll mean it."

"Yes, sir."

I wished I could get sleepy, but I just pretended. I had to do that when Mom was gone, because I didn't sleep much, but if Dad found out I was awake, he'd try to stay up with me. Then he'd get all tired and grumpy and I'd feel guilty.

So I pretended until he carried me to bed and tucked me in. Then I waited until I heard his door close, and waited a little longer, until I saw his light click off and the hallway go dark. Then I got up and pushed my own door closed, snuck back across my bedroom, turned on my little desk lamp, picked up my Crazy List, and opened up my laptop.

One by one, I picked out the items on the list and did some searches. Okay, okay. Ghosts at the Abrams farm were probably a stretch. But I looked up everything I could find on hallucinations, and I didn't think I was hallucinating when I saw all that stuff.

Wikipedia said, "A hallucination is a perception in

the absence of apparent stimulus that has qualities of real perception."

Huh? Did Angel write definitions for these people?

The rest of the article explained that hallucinations could come from seizures and infections and drugs and falling asleep when you thought you were awake and migraines and staying in dark rooms too long and brain tumors. I rubbed the sides of my head. Brain tumor. That would be my luck. I clicked on another article.

About halfway down, I found "Flashbacks vs. Hallucinations," looked up "flashback," and read aloud, "A sudden, usually powerful, re-experiencing of a past experience or elements of a past experience." Wikipedia again. Yep. Angel had a job waiting for her in the future, writing articles for Wikipedia.

I read about flashbacks on two other sites and figured out that the word meant reliving bad stuff from the past. That made me think of Captain Armstrong, when he thought he was back in the desert still fighting in the war but he was really standing in his driveway trying to pick up his newspaper, remembering scary things.

Except, how could I be remembering something I had never seen?

My head hurt.

Maybe I did have a brain tumor.

I clicked off the web browser and uploaded the pictures of the Abrams farm to get my mind off hallucinations and flashbacks and Captain Armstrong and scary war things and brain tumors, but they didn't help much. They reminded me of disaster movies where the camera sweeps across endless fields of everything splatted and exploded. The only thing missing was the doomy-boomy music.

Most of the shots captured ashes and melted stuff. All the black char made me shiver.

Fire. The farm, burning. Cissy and Mom . . . What did I see?

Those flecks—

I shivered, then rubbed my eyes to make that image go away. I had to rub my ears, too, because they were buzzing again.

When I looked up, all I could see were my closed white blinds. I was sitting at the desk in front of my bedroom window, but I always kept the blinds closed and the windows shut at night. I couldn't shake the feeling that something would jump through the darkness and get me.

Was that normal? I picked at the bows on my nightgown. *Am I on the way to getting sick like Mom?*

No. I smacked my ears until the buzzing stopped. Not happening. Not going crazy. I was fine.

But I saw things at the Abrams farm. Images that couldn't have been real.

Maybe they were real. Maybe they were flashbacks, not hallucinations.

"No," I said out loud this time. I had to rub my arms to keep from shivering again. It was stupid, feeling so cold when it was spring in Mississippi and already hot even with air-conditioning.

I clicked through a few more pictures. More ashes. More soot. I printed the first one and made a note on it.

These ashes might have dead people in them. That's gross. And kind of sad.

The next picture was the same, and the one after that and the one after that. I didn't know how journalists and detectives did it, looking at pictures of crime scenes over and over again. These shots only had burned-up wood and farm tools, not bodies and blood or horrible stuff, and my brain already didn't want to keep studying them. Maybe I wasn't cut out for journalism, either.

I ticked through pictures of skeleton house boards

and scorched trees, then some shots of the area closer to the woods. Normal trees. Grass so green, it almost hurt my eyes. Then I found the corner of Angel's pink dress, and one image of her sunburned knee. We were thorough investigators—but effective? Not so much. We had a long way to go before we'd be one of those teams people made television shows about.

I shivered all over again when I got to the picture of the brush where I thought I had seen someone hiding, right after my hallucination or flashback or whatever that had been. There was nothing in the brush but trees and leaves. So that wasn't real either. It was just me being chicken about stuff jumping at me through the darkness.

It wasn't something I talked about much, being scared of the dark. More like what was in the dark that I couldn't see. I always thought something had to be there, something awful and dangerous that vanished when I finally made it to a switch and flooded the world with light. Sometimes it was hardest and scariest to see what was right there beside you—what had been there right beside you all along, waiting to snarl and bite you and eat you whole.

My chest got tight from just thinking about how it felt to get stuck in a dark room and have to run for a switch. "I'm a great big baby," I muttered, tempted to turn off my lamp and pull up my blinds and make myself stare out the window into the night until I just got over it.

I had tried that before, lots of times, and it never worked. But I kept doing it whenever I could find the courage, because maybe the next time I'd make it past the panic and I wouldn't be a baby anymore.

When I stood, my legs shook. I glanced at the picture of the brush where nobody was hiding, then switched off the lamp. Then I went and opened the blinds really fast, before I could wimp out. The second they opened, I stepped toward the desk.

Well?

If something did jump out of the darkness and bust through my window like a rabid fire-breathing lizard on a rampage, I wanted to give it some space.

Quiet pressed into my ears as I stared out the inky glass. If Mom had been home, she would have had the television on in their bedroom, watching true-crime documentaries or gathering recipes off cooking channels. Sometimes she listened to music, and sometimes she played movies. Silence was never a problem when Mom was here.

But Mom's not here. I hated that so much. Tears tickled my eyelids, but I ground my teeth until they went away. I had already cried enough after I got home, and Dad said Mom would be gone for a while.

A moth smacked against the window, and I almost peed myself. I said something I'd get grounded for if Dad heard me, and closed the blinds as fast as I could. It took a minute before I could breathe enough to stalk back to my desk, click on my lamp, and throw myself into the chair. Still a baby. That completely sucked.

I squinted at the picture of the brush, too ticked off for words—then I squinted harder. My fingers flicked across the laptop keyboard as I pulled the picture into the edit window, cropped it, and magnified it. Again.

And one more time.

I couldn't be totally sure, but right at the edge of the brush where I thought I had seen somebody standing, Angel had snapped a photo of a shoe. It looked like a black tennis shoe, the kind grown men wore.

I sent the photo to Peavine's phone with the note *that look like a shoe 2 u??*

Almost immediately, his text tone sang out, and I read, *Kinda. Whaddya thnk?*

sumbdy wz watchn.

Who?

dnt knw. the serial killer?

A few seconds went by, then Peavine texted that he had to go to bed.

My eyes shifted from the phone to the picture to the window. My stupid baby brain told me the darkness outside was just like a poisonous copperhead, trying to slither around the edges of my blinds to bite me. Would it get me put in some hospital in Memphis if I glued the blinds to the sill?

Peavine's mom was great, but I wished she would let him stay up later and talk to me. What should we do with the picture? If I showed it to Dad, he probably wouldn't think it was anything important. It was just a shoe. I couldn't even see if there was a leg in it. It might have been a shoe with no person attached to it at all. It wasn't like the police could do anything with a photo of a shoe, right?

What would a good journalist do to make sense out of this mess?

A good journalist would write.

But I didn't know what to write. I didn't even know where to start.

Finally, I opened a document to the side of the photos

and typed a list of what I knew for sure about the Abrams case:

1. Old Mr. Abrams got shot, and nobody knows who shot him.
2. The Abrams farm got burned to the ground, and nobody knows who set the fire.
3. Cissy and Doc might be dead or alive, and nobody knows where they are.

After I stared at it a while, I added some possibilities.

4. Mom might have been there.
5. I might have been there.
6. Somebody might have been watching us while we searched.
7. I might be crazy.

Great. Peavine and Angel and I had gone to the farm to search for clues and solve some of the mystery, but we ended up finding nothing but more questions.

I closed the computer lid, switched on the night-light near the foot of my bed, then turned off the lamp. To prove I wasn't a complete baby, I sat there studying the blinds, making sure the darker darkness didn't try to get inside.

After a while I got in my bed. Then I got back out of my bed, took my pillow and blanket, and got under the bed instead. For some reason, I didn't want to close my eyes. I didn't want to sleep. I definitely didn't want to dream about anything. What if the dreams turned into hallucinations and I couldn't wake up? What if—

"Mom?" I tried to breathe but coughed instead. My room smelled like something on fire.

I got out of bed too fast, tangled my feet in my bedspread, and fell to my knees. My hair swung against my cheeks, making me shiver. It was wet. Why was my hair wet? It wasn't a bath night.

"Mom?" I got up and fought my way out of the bedspread. The muscles in my belly hurt, like the time I lifted Dad's weights too many times. Nobody met me in the hall outside my room. Silence hung like smoke in the house. No television. No Mom. No Dad.

My heart thumped in my throat, making it hard to swallow. I ran to the hall light switch and flipped it on. Yellow light blazed in a long strip, but darkness still crowded out of my bedroom and the guest bathroom and my parents' room. Fast as I could, I turned on those switches too.

"Mom!"

Nobody answered. My ears hurt from listening. I shoved open the door to the master bathroom, but nobody was there, either. The closet—no people in there. Out in the hall again, I ran to the kitchen.

Where was Mom? Dad should be home.

Lights. I had to turn them on. Kitchen. Pantry. Living room. Basement. I hit the switch at the top of the stairs, and something rattled down below.

I froze.

Air whistled through my teeth. My fingers dug into my palms. The muscles in my throat ached from wanting to yell for Mom again.

But what if that's not Mom . . .

Downstairs in the basement, a door closed.

I backed up so fast, I tripped over my nightgown and pitched backward—

My eyes popped open as I swung my arms, trying to keep my balance.

I was standing totally still in the dark, in front of the kitchen sink. A whimper slipped out as I jumped forward and flicked on the light to break the blackness before it reached for me.

What was I doing in the kitchen?

As I eased down from my toes where I had stretched to hit the light switch, my heel ground into something wet that crinkled. I jumped and picked up my foot.

One of my school drinks lay on the floor, where I had crushed the pouch. Nothing much was left in it, though, or it would have made a bigger mess . . . to go along with the chip wrappers and pieces of bread on the floor.

Had I been eating in my sleep? I had heard of sleep-walking, but sleep-eating? Really? My heart slowly moved from gallop to trot, then on down to walk. Little by little, I managed to breathe normally, even though I couldn't tell if my belly was bigger than usual.

I had completely trashed the kitchen in my sleep.

I glanced toward the hall but didn't see Dad's light. I hadn't turned on the hall light, like I did in my dream. Could people hallucinate in dreams? Were dreams just hallucinations anyway?

Of course I dreamed all of that—it hadn't been real, any more than what I imagined I saw at the Abrams farm. I mean, bits and pieces of it, maybe. My thoughts felt cramped and muddled, so I rubbed the sides of my face.

Nothing came clear.

I looked at the clock on the stove. The only thing I knew for sure was, I needed to clean up the kitchen as fast as I could, because here in not-dream-totally-real-world, it was almost time for Dad's alarm to buzz.

From the Notebook of Detective Peavine Jones

Interview of Armstrong, Cory J., CPT USAR, Eleven Days After the Fire
Location: Captain Armstrong's House, with Lemonade
Everything is really, really, really clean in here. It's kind of weird.

Captain Armstrong: You two know it's really early, right?
Footer: Sure, but I know you get out pretty early to run, before it gets too hot.
Captain Armstrong: Well, come on in. I'll get you some lemonade. How's your mom, Footer? Hear anything yet?
Footer: No, sir.
Captain Armstrong: You two are pretty tough kids. You do well, for your mom being sick, and you, Peavine, with your dad leaving and all. I'm proud of both of you.
Me: Thank you, sir. Could you tell us a little about flashbacks?
Captain Armstrong: [suspect looks

surprised.] That's a strange question. I thought I was pretending to be a suspect in the Abrams fire.

Footer: I read about flashbacks on the Internet, and—

Captain Armstrong: Don't fill your heads full of that crap you can read online. Look, it's no secret I got problems from the war, so I guess it's natural that you come to me if you're curious about it. But why?

Footer: If people see something really bad, like a murder and a fire, could they get flashbacks?

Captain Armstrong: I'm sure they could. Lots of traumatized people out there, because the world has gone totally [censored] insane. Oh, uh, sorry about the language.

Footer: What caused your flashbacks?

Captain Armstrong: Describing my time in the service is hard, Footer. Sometimes when I talk about what happened to me in Afghanistan, or see pictures that remind me of the war, or hear certain sounds or smell certain smells, I relive the worst of what I went through over there.

Footer: Oh. I'm sorry. I didn't know that, sir. Thank you for your service to our country.

Captain Armstrong: You're welcome. But you don't have to apologize for asking.

Footer: What I really want to know is, with your flashbacks and stuff, have you ever realized you forgot something important, like a really, really bad thing you saw?

Captain Armstrong: Yeah. That's part of it. But I always remember it later, usually at the worst possible moment. [Suspect leans forward. Journalist leans back, probably because suspect is so tall, and sort of scary with that glare.] War isn't like on television or in the movies. Even when they get it right on film, you can't smell the blood or taste the sand scraping your face or feel the desert sun trying to cook your brain to dust in your skull.

Footer: [Journalist looks a little green.] I see. Okay. But if you wanted to remember what you forgot, is there any way to set a flashback off on purpose—you know, to make yourself remember?

Captain Armstrong: I never want to remember. None of us do.

Footer: [Journalist is quiet for so long, I almost start talking, but she stops me.] One more question, sir.

Captain Armstrong: I'm listening.

Footer: Do you always wear those black shoes when you run?

Captain Armstrong: [Suspect stares at his own feet.] Yeah. Why?

Footer: Just wondered. Thanks! [Journalist leaves the house so fast, I have to hustle to keep up with her.]

What I Did Over the Weekend

Footer Davis
2nd Period
Ms. Malone

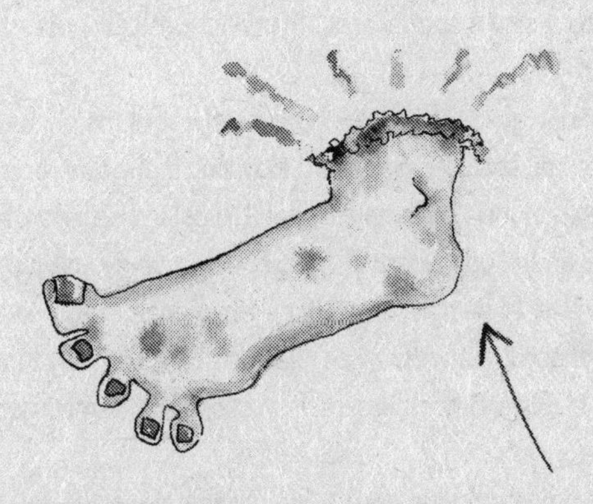

This is a copperhead snake-bit rotten foot that had to get cut off. I didn't have to get my foot cut off, because Mom saved me.

Instead, I interviewed murder suspects and had to clean snake guts off the bird feeders Sunday evening. Some of the guts were the same color as my hair. That's gross. The houseflies on the snake guts were more gross.

Now that I know houseflies eat snake guts, I don't want them crawling on my head.

I might have to move to Alaska. They don't have many houseflies. They don't have many worms, either. Alaska would be the best place ever, except for the whole sixty-degrees-below-zero-in-the-winter thing. Oh, and walruses. I saw a special about them last week. Walruses kind of freak me out.

Mom had to go to the hospital because she shot the snake and almost broke her shoulder. She didn't stay long in the emergency room, because they sent her to Memphis. I want to go see her soon, but I'm not allowed to go on the unit where she stays. Being eleven years old sucks. When I'm twelve, I'll be able to visit Mom when she's sick. I hope she doesn't forget about me while I can't see her. Plus, Dad only knows how to cook fish sticks and hamburgers. Fish sticks and hamburgers get icky after a while.

Peavine, Angel, and ~~me~~ I went to the Abrams place. We didn't find much. Angel says the ashes have dead people in them. That freaks me out almost as much as walruses.

C+
Needs more organization—and this was supposed to be two pages. Nice try. Also, illustrations really aren't necessary. I'm glad no one was injured by the snake, and I'm sorry about your mom.
PS I have never been fond of walruses myself. They're gigantic and wrinkly, and they look like they accidentally stuck straws up their noses.

CHAPTER 5

Eleven Days After the Fire

Hot-for-spring turned into wicked hot by Tuesday morning, and the air conditioner at school stopped working by lunch, and my yellow blouse kept sticking to my back. I wanted school to let out for the summer already, but we still had seven weeks to go.

I didn't get much sleep Saturday night, or Sunday night either, because my stomach hurt after I went back to bed. I worried about sleep-eating, and a little bit about the shoe picture. I didn't worry about the barrette Angel found. That could have been anybody's. So what if Mom got new barrettes after the fire? That didn't mean she had lost her old ones. And even if she did lose her old barrettes, that didn't mean she was over at the Abrams farm the night it burned.

None of that stuff had been real.

Hurry.

That's what Mom said to Cissy Abrams in that sort-of-hallucination or flashback or whatever it was. And then the other dream, where I woke up alone, after a bath I didn't remember, smelling smoke even though there was no fire in my house. . . . I had to be losing it. I barely got all that food mess cleaned up before Dad came in to make breakfast.

Peavine thought we should send Angel's shoe picture to the MBI, since they thought Cissy and Doc might still be alive and kidnapped, and maybe the shoe was on the foot of a serial killer stalker creep who was watching us to make sure we didn't discover the right clues to blow up all his plans.

Captain Armstrong has shoes just like that.

That kind of freaks me out, but Peavine says a lot of people have black running shoes and I shouldn't jump to conclusions. He's probably right. Captain Armstrong is too nice to murder anybody.

I just needed to find the MBI's e-mail address and do it when I got home. I glanced at Peavine from two rows back, tasting and retasting the peanut-butter-and-jelly sandwich I had at lunch. His white T-shirt looked as sweaty as my shirt.

I gripped the sides of my book. Sweat trickled down my neck on both sides as I went back to staring at a black-and-white photo of pantyhose crumpled next to a box full of people parts. That was pretty disgusting. All around me, pencils scratched out the assignment I had already finished.

My eyes narrowed at the photo.

Cissy Abrams, looking dead . . .

Those awful black flecks . . .

My mom, wide-eyed as I fell . . .

Waking up, smelling the world on fire . . .

I got out of bed the night everything happened. I remember doing that. The house was so motionless and silent, it scared me, so that much of my dream had been real. I remembered running to turn on lights, but my folks never left me alone.

Pushing open doors to dark rooms and digging for light switches . . .

The stench of fire and smoke . . .

Noises in the basement . . .

"*The A to Z Dictionary of Serial Killers*, Miss Davis?" Ms. Malone's voice scared me so bad, I let go of the book. My teacher pulled the heavy volume out of my slack grip. I blinked fast, trying to be in now instead of that bad, burning night.

Ms. Malone glanced at the pictures of the pantyhose and the box, and she frowned. Her back straightened, and I could swear she was getting taller. She had her ebony hair pulled back from her face and fastened behind her head so smooth and tight, her eyes slanted at the corners. Her big tortoiseshell glasses frames made her pupils look gigantic as she leveled her *I do not approve* stare squarely at my face. "This wasn't exactly what I had in mind when I gave you permission to further your literary acumen if you finished your test early. Care to explain why you didn't get a novel from our reading shelf, or where you got, ah, *this* bit of inappropriateness?"

She lifted the book I had checked out of the public library last week, using Dad's library card, swearing to the librarian he needed it for his work. My brain stumbled back and forth between fuzzy images I didn't know if I was remembering or imagining and how much trouble I'd be in when Ms. Malone called the library, then ratted me out to my parents. I knew I needed to say something quick, but I just sat there like a big duh, staring at my favorite teacher. I couldn't see Peavine because Ms. Malone was standing between us, but I could tell he had stopped writing. Everyone had. The room had gone as silent as my house on the night of the fire.

I clasped my hands and squeezed so they would stop shaking. Ms. Malone was still staring at me, waiting. Life would have been a lot easier if I could have beamed myself to some distant planet and lived out my days hunting alien mutant rock eaters, like in one of Angel's books. My brain kept flashing one of those monsters like a neon sign, along with an arrow and a caption.

I couldn't help it. It was all I could see, so I couldn't

Alien mutant rock eater. It's so ugly, it's cute, bless its heart.

say anything to Ms. Malone, because if I said something, it would be about alien mutant rock eaters, and that would be bad.

The old intercom over the chalkboard crackled, and a woman's voice said, "Classroom five?"

Ms. Malone didn't take her eyes off me. "Yes?"

"I'm sending Ms. Perry to cover," one of the office secretaries said. "Please report to Main with Fontana Davis."

The alien mutant rock eaters in my brain exploded, and my mouth came open as the whole class went, "*Oooo-ooooh.*" Even Ms. Malone looked surprised. The office hardly ever interrupted class, unless somebody was in bad trouble or something awful had happened.

Mom? My belly drew so tight, my ribs ached.

Ms. Malone snapped the serial-killer dictionary closed and tucked it under her arm. When she looked at me with a question in her expression, I shrugged and shook my head. My neck felt like concrete.

"Well," was all Ms. Malone had time to say before Ms. Perry walked in and we had to go.

When I stood and started walking, my legs and arms felt numb. I didn't let myself glance at Peavine as I passed his desk, but I heard him sniff like he was worried.

When we got out into the hall, Ms. Malone glanced back at me, and she stopped walking. "Footer, you okay?"

I nodded, but she didn't start walking again. The cream-colored tile under my feet seemed to grab my eyeballs and yank my head down. I didn't want to see anyone right that second. The only thing I really wanted to do was throw up. I studied the sunlight shining in from the hall windows, and the black line of dirt that ran along the base of our purple lockers, right where nobody could sweep.

"Footer." Ms. Malone knelt beside me, still holding on to my book about serial killers. Her free hand rested on my shoulder. "You've lost every bit of color in your face. Are you going to faint?"

That made me look at her. "Fainting's for sissies."

Ms. Malone's face was right in front of mine. Her dark

skin looked smooth and perfect. I smelled the peppermint she always ate while sitting at her desk as we worked on our papers. Her eyes seemed twice as gigantic up close, but they also seemed nice.

She smiled at me. "Lots of people faint. It's about blood pressure and medical issues, not being a sissy. But you already look better. Want to tell me what's scaring you?"

"No."

She didn't stop smiling, but her eyes dimmed, like maybe she was sad. "You afraid this is about your mom?"

The pain in my stomach got so sharp, I wrapped my arms around my middle. I belched peanut butter and jelly but swallowed it. "Yeah. A little."

"Okay." Ms. Malone stood, keeping her hand on my shoulder. "Then let's go see. I'll be right there with you, no matter what."

Like that would help. I let out a breath as the pain eased, and my hands quit shaking. Actually, it did help, knowing Ms. Malone would be there. At least a little. That was kind of weird.

We had to walk down two long hallways, turn a corner, and walk up one flight of stairs to get to the main office. Every step seemed to take too long. When we finally arrived, the glass walls were so lined with plants that I couldn't really see who was waiting for us inside, only that it wasn't Dad, unless he was sitting down, because Dad was taller than the plants.

Ms. Malone went first through the door, and I came in behind her to see the office secretary, Ms. Starling, who was standing in front of one of the conference rooms with a woman I didn't know. Ms. Starling was skinny and old, but the stranger looked like she might be a soccer star. She had dark brown eyes—wide, not warm and kind like Ms. Malone's. Her hair was a bright shade of blond that didn't look natural, and she was very tan. Peavine and Angel, they were real blonds. Peavine got freckles if he stayed out in the sun, and Angel got burned. This woman was a fake, or at least her hair was.

She had on a brown skirt, pink heels, and a pink sweater with no sleeves. A name badge hung on a lanyard around her neck, but it was turned around backward, so all I could see was a happy-face sticker somebody had pressed onto the plastic sleeve.

"Fontana, this is Stephanie Bridges," Ms. Starling said in her crackly voice, gesturing at pink-sweater-high-heels lady. I swear it sounded like Ms. Starling was still talking through the old intercom speakers. "She's from DFCS. That's the Mississippi Department of Human Services, Division of Family and Children Services. She needs to talk to you."

"Why?" I glanced around Stephanie Bridges, into the open conference room. Nobody was there. The shaking in my hands came back double. "Where's my dad?" I hated how squeaky I sounded. "Shouldn't he be here if I'm going to get interviewed by someone from a government agency?"

"No," Ms. Starling said.

Ms. Malone frowned at her. "Don't they need a parent's consent, at least?"

"DFCS doesn't need permission to speak to a child," said the voice that came through our speakers every morning. "We've done this before. I know the rules."

Ms. Malone kept frowning. Stephanie Bridges smiled at me the way people do right before they pop out with *Bless your heart*.

I wished I was an alien mutant rock eater who lived on any planet but this one. I didn't want to go in that room with Stephanie Bridges. I didn't want to talk to anyone with fake hair and a smile she didn't really mean. Her heels were so high, they reminded me of walrus tusks. How did she even walk in those shoes without snapping every bone in her ankles?

Anything that reminded me of walruses had to be a bad omen.

"Um, no thanks." I shook my head. If I ran for it and turned right, the massive row of plants around the front door would give me some cover as I bolted down the hall.

"You have to do this," Ms. Starling said.

"I do not. I want my dad." I backed up a little. Ms. Malone went with me, like she knew I was thinking about making a break for it.

"Fontana—" Stephanie Bridges started, but I cut her off.

"I go by Footer."

She glanced down at her papers and made a note. "Okay, Footer. I don't want this to be hard or scary. I just need to ask you some questions."

Her accent was way southern, like mine. She looked big-city, but she sounded like home. That was something, at least.

"Why do you need to ask me questions?" My heart pounded and pounded. I wasn't sure I was breathing.

"Because some people are concerned that you might be in danger." The fake smile came back.

Pound, pound, pound . . . I wanted to hide behind the plants. "What people?" My voice sounded like a mouse whistle.

"Are you new at this?" Ms. Malone asked Stephanie Bridges.

"What?" The woman stopped smiling. Ms. Starling shook her head and tottered off, muttering something about a society doomed by no discipline.

"I—yes. I'm early in my career," Stephanie Bridges admitted.

Ms. Malone's frown eased. She kept her arms folded, though. "How long have you been out of school?"

"I don't think that's relevant," Stephanie Bridges said, but she looked at her feet like I always did when I knew I was in trouble with Ms. Malone.

Breathe. My chest moved up and down, and I felt a little better.

"Footer, this lady has a job to do," Ms. Malone said without taking her gaze off Stephanie Bridges. "Come on. I'll go in with you."

"I'm sorry, that's not allowed." Stephanie Bridges shook her head.

Ms. Malone gave her the same glare she always used to hush me when I was making her mad. "Do you want to get this done or not?"

Stephanie Bridges pressed her lips shut, turning her whole mouth into a straight line.

"I'll stay right with you, Footer." Ms. Malone took my hand. "You can stop anytime you want."

Stephanie Bridges spoke so quietly that her voice was nearly a whisper. "But I have to interview Fontana in private."

"I'm going in with *Footer*," Ms. Malone said. "If you have an issue with that, take it up with whomever you'd like." She looked at me with her big, nice eyes. "Ready?"

She squeezed my hand.

I nodded, and we went into the conference room together.

Stephanie Bridges followed and closed the door behind us so hard, she rattled the glass panes on either side.

CHAPTER 6

Eleven Days After the Fire. What Does This Woman Want?

The conference table was long and square, and I sat on one side with Ms. Malone. Stephanie Bridges came and plopped down beside me, so I got up and went all the way to the end, where the chairs had been pushed every which way. I sat on one that wasn't against the table.

Ms. Malone gave Stephanie Bridges a look I couldn't read, then came to where I was and sat next to me again. Relief helped me breathe a little better.

Stephanie Bridges stared at me for a second. I looked away from her and studied the cream-colored cinderblock walls and pictures of previous principals and football teams. A room air conditioner hummed in one curtained window, making the fabric ripple. Outside the conference room, a few people moved around in the office, but I couldn't hear them. All I could focus on was my own breathing and the rustle of papers as Stephanie Bridges moved her notes around on the smudged wood.

Finally, she stood, slid me a card with her name and number on it, and then sat again.

I thought about balling up the card and throwing it at the wall, but to be polite I put it in my jeans pocket. I could always pitch it when I got home. Besides, I wanted her name and number to give Dad, so he could tell this woman not to talk to me again without him.

Stephanie Bridges said, "Your mother was taken to Memphis this weekend, to the New Dawn program. Do you know what that is?"

The sticky-sweet sound in her voice made me curl my fingers into fists. "It's a psychiatric unit. Mom has a mental illness called bipolar disorder. Her brain chemicals make her mood get too high or too low, and sometimes her thinking gets confused. When she takes her medicine, she does okay. When she doesn't, she has problems and has to go to the hospital until she's better."

I stopped talking, and the only sound in the room was the steady hum of the air conditioner.

"I see." Stephanie Bridges briefly looked stunned. Then she made a few notes on her papers. "And when your mother has these problems, who takes care of you?"

"Dad." I fidgeted with the fabric-covered chair arm. The chair had wheels. It was hard not to start rolling around.

"Doesn't your father work?"

"Of course he does. But when Mom's sick, he changes his schedule so he's home when I'm home. If he can't be there, I stay with Peavine and Angel until he's able to pick me up. Ms. Jones doesn't have to work all the time, because she got a lot of money when her aunt died, and then she won some in a lottery. Ms. Jones is a great mom."

Something like jealousy poked me in the belly as I said that, and I got all distracted thinking about how Ms. Jones was completely normal and Mom wasn't, and how Angel and Peavine didn't ever have to worry about Ms. Jones shooting snakes and getting DCFS called and ending up in a hospital.

Stephanie Bridges kept her head down and made more notes. "So you're never left unattended?"

Dark rooms in a quiet house . . . I kept my voice completely level and calm. "I am never left unattended."

Liar.

Dang. I didn't want to be lying right now. Lying brought me bad luck, and I didn't need any more of that in my life. And what was all of this about, anyway? Could it be about the Abrams farm? I already talked to the police the morning after the fire. I told them I didn't see anything or know anything.

Liar!

From somewhere deep in my mind, the ghost of Cissy Abrams stared at me with those blank, hollow eyes.

Stephanie Bridges was talking again. "Tell me what you understand about what prompted your mother's latest hospitalization."

I blinked at her, trying to make myself act right.

Ms. Malone poked the arm of my chair. "Tell her why your mom went to the hospital, Footer. And be nice."

"She hurt her shoulder and had to go to the emergency room to get it taken care of." I shrugged like that was no big deal. "She really hates doctors, so that probably upset her."

"Is she easily upset?" Stephanie Bridges asked.

"Not always." *Liar, liar! Bad luck!* "Well, sometimes."

The woman narrowed her eyes. "Has she ever gotten angry with you when she was upset?"

"Well, sure." I picked at the chair arm. "But I deserved it."

Stephanie Bridges scribbled a note. The triumphant look on her face made me lean forward. "I mean it. I really deserved it. Sometimes I do stupid stuff. Like, I accidentally lit the backyard on fire trying an experiment with a magnifying glass."

The DCFS woman looked up slowly, her pen frozen in her hand. "You set a fire?"

Doom crashed over me like a cold wave. I wanted to fall out of my chair and die.

Ms. Malone cleared her throat. "You mean the experiment in *Superspy* magazine?"

"Yes, ma'am." I tore my gaze away from Stephanie Bridges and looked at Ms. Malone instead.

Ms. Malone's expression was relaxed, and her eyes seemed as nice as ever. "Did you use too many newspapers?"

"Way too many."

The heat in my face faded as Ms. Malone nodded. "I did that too. Driveway still has a black spot."

We both looked at the DCFS worker, who didn't seem to know what to say next. She finally came up with "What does your mother do when she's angry with you?"

"She tells me not to do stupid stuff like accidentally setting the backyard on fire." I smiled at Stephanie Bridges. When she didn't smile back, I said, "Sometimes she yells it?"

Would that make her happy? What did she want, anyway? Me, I wanted to get out of that conference room and go back to class, then go home and lie in my bed and think without anybody bothering me. Being interviewed sucked. Maybe Peavine and I shouldn't interview any more people because it sucked so bad. We were probably earning ourselves barrels and barrels of rotten luck. Who wanted to answer hard questions like this?

"Has your mother ever hit you?" Stephanie Bridges asked like she was reading from a list of dumb questions she made up before she ever met me.

"No."

"Has she ever threatened to hurt you in any way?"

"No."

"Has she ever put you in danger?"

"Mom would never do that." The tips of my fingers dug into the chair arms. "She worries about me all the time. She hurt her shoulder trying to be sure a snake didn't bite me."

At this, Stephanie Bridges brightened, and that doomed feeling washed over me again. "She shot the snake with your father's largest firearm."

Firearm? This woman and Angel would get along well. I wondered if she was going to start babbling about well-organized militias. "Yes. The Nitro. It's an elephant gun."

Stephanie Bridges scribbled on her paper some more, then locked eyes with me. "Did she have any training to use that weapon safely?"

"Who has training to use an elephant gun? I mean in this country. I'm sure people in Africa and India might get training, since elephants actually live there." I shook my head. "I don't even know why they make elephant guns, because elephants are endangered, and nobody's supposed to shoot them. They should make walrus guns. Walrus guns would make a lot more sense."

"I agree," Ms. Malone said. When Stephanie Bridges stared at her, she added, "It's the tusks," and shivered.

Stephanie Bridges seemed to consider this but then

decided to ignore it. "Your father has quite a collection of dangerous firearms, doesn't he, Font—I mean Footer?"

She was starting to make me really mad, with all her stupid questions and stupid words. "I hear your accent. You're not from any great-big city up north or out west, right?"

"I—uh, no. I'm from Jackson." Her cheeks got red around the edges.

I tapped my fingers on the table a few times, then tried to be nice again. "Jackson's big enough, I guess."

"Big enough for what?" She looked confused.

"To mess up your brain so you say 'firearm' instead of 'gun.'"

Now she looked really confused, and her cheeks got a bunch more red. Ms. Malone was smiling a little, and I could tell she was trying not to smile a whole lot. After coughing a few times, Stephanie Bridges came up with "'Firearm' is the proper term. They teach us to use proper terms."

I stared at her. "Where? In DFCS worker school or something?"

"In social work school, and in our training classes." Her face was all kinds of red now. That should have made me feel guilty, but it didn't. "It's supposed to make things more clear, and easier when we interview people."

"It doesn't make it easier for me," I told her. "It just sounds stupid."

"Okay," she said. "I'll try again. Does your dad have a big gun collection?"

She didn't look mad yet. She didn't sound mad either. Did I want her to be mad? Probably not. Only I did, a little bit.

"Dad was a soldier," I said. "Now he's a policeman. Of course he has guns, but he keeps them locked in the gun case and gun safe so they aren't dangerous. I never shoot them unless he's with me, except for my BB gun."

The woman's eyes got round. "You have a BB gun?"

Oh, great. "Yes. And safety glasses, and a certificate from the class I took at the sheriff's department to learn to use it safely."

This seemed to surprise her. "But aren't you a little young to have any kind of gun?"

"You didn't have any brothers, did you?" Ms. Malone asked, only it wasn't really a question. "It's a BB gun. It barely makes holes in cans."

"You could shoot out your eye with that!" Stephanie Bridges almost yelled, and I wanted to bang my head on the conference table. "And no, I didn't have brothers. It was just my mother and me, but I don't see how that matters."

"Sure you could shoot your eye out with a BB gun," I said. "If you were stupid enough not to wear your safety glasses and stare into the barrel while you were shooting it, which would be hard, because it's kind of long, and if

I put my eye on the barrel, I probably couldn't reach the trigger. Are you going to tell Dad you came to talk to me? Because I'm calling him about it the second you leave."

Stephanie Bridges looked back at her papers and made a few more notes, letting the room get quiet around the air-conditioner hum. Then she said, "I'm not sure it's a good idea to have guns in the house with children and a person who has mental illness."

I sighed. "I told you, they're locked."

"Your mother opened the case," she said. "How?"

The dull *beat-beat* of my heart made me bite my bottom lip. I so wanted this to be over, and I so didn't want to answer this question. I thought about the gun case down in our big basement. There was a pool table down there too, and a television, and Dad's weights, and a little bedroom with a bathroom and shower but no windows. I wanted to be down there right at that moment, watching movies and lifting Dad's hand weights instead of talking to this woman.

"How did your mother open the gun case, Footer?" Stephanie Bridges asked again.

"She bent the lock. Look, I have to go to the restroom," I said. "And it's almost lunchtime. Are we done?"

Stephanie Bridges shifted her gaze to Ms. Malone, then seemed to process the title of the serial-killer book Ms. Malone was holding. "Are you teaching *that* in the classroom?"

"I took it up from a student," Ms. Malone said.

"Which student?"

Ms. Malone gave her the best smile I had ever seen. "Footer asked if you were finished."

Stephanie Bridges eyed her and the book, and then she eyed me. "For now," she finally said. "But I may have more questions later."

CHAPTER 7

Still Eleven Days After the Fire, but a Lot Happened, So It Feels Like Months. I Really Hate Days Like This.

I'd probably be a good journalist, because when I can't stand stuff anymore and my brain does its freeze-frames, nothing matters more than the words. Like the conversation with Ms. Malone, after Stephanie Bridges finally went away:

> **Ms. Malone:** I'll take the serial-killer book back to the public library. Why were you reading it?
> **Me:** Because *Dateline* said maybe a serial killer kidnapped Cissy and Doc Abrams. I wanted to see if any of the guys in that book kidnapped kids.
> **Ms. Malone:** This is where I'm supposed to lecture you about not messing around the

Abrams farm because it could be dangerous, then get annoyed because you're saying "Yes, ma'am" but really ignoring me.

Me: Yes, ma'am

Ms. Malone: Footer, while Ms. Bridges is involved with your family, I wouldn't light any fires with magnifying glasses or poke around those ashes or check out any more books about serial killers. She might get the wrong idea.

Me: Yes, ma'am.

I remembered it all, but it was snips and snaps, with words in the picture instead of faces. No other sights, no other sounds, no other feelings. Snip, snap.

"What'd your dad say when you called?" Peavine asked me a few hours later, at recess.

"He was ticked." I wiped sweat off my forehead with my arm, then scrubbed my arm on my shirt. "He's checking with people. He said we'd talk when he gets home tonight."

We were standing under the maple tree near the back of the sixth-grade wing. We could see Angel's class out behind their wing, and across the street from the third graders a bunch of teachers were coming and going from the convenience store and fast-food restaurants, carrying sacks. There was a guy standing out beside the store too.

"Your dad and the doctors going to let you go to the hospital tomorrow after school?" Peavine asked.

"I threw a big fit this morning about seeing Mom, so probably." I studied the guy at the store. He had on jeans and a red plaid shirt with the sleeves cut off. He had to be about to melt in this heat. His hair was dark and short, but he was too far away for me to make out more details. He stood near the store's door eating a sandwich, as if he wanted to seem like he was minding his own business and having lunch, but I knew he was watching the playground.

Here was a suspicious stranger if I ever saw one.

"Look," I told Peavine, nodding toward the store. "That guy is creeping me out. Just what we needed in Bugtussle. Wood lice, snakes, a fire, missing kids, my mother, a serial killer—and now a creep. We should maybe interview him."

"Great," Peavine muttered, like he was the one catching a creep at work, but then I glanced toward where he was pointing. Angel was standing near the corner of the third-grade wing. She had on a yellow dress covered in long ribbons. She also had one of her thick books clutched against her chest, and a ring of kids around her. The teachers were halfway behind the other corner, so they couldn't see what was happening.

Peavine started forward, swinging his legs with a vengeance.

"She hates it when you help her," I called after him.

"Yeah, well, too bad," he shot back.

I followed. The kids around Angel didn't see us coming. When we got there, the boy in front, a grimy little bully named Max Selwin, pushed Angel backward. Her shoulders hit the red brick wall.

"Gimme the book, freak," Max said.

Angel stared at the ground and shook her head. "No."

"I said, give it here."

"No!"

Peavine didn't stop at the line of kids. He shouldered right through them. They scattered sideways, letting me through too. Max raised his hand to grab Angel's book, but Peavine hit him in the elbow with his crutch.

"Ow!" Max grabbed his arm and whirled to face us. He had to look up to go eye to eye with Peavine, and that only seemed to make the kid madder.

"Oh, good." His dirt-smeared face twisted into a sneer. "It's the freak's crippled brother."

Max laughed. Nobody else did. I stopped beside Peavine, fists raised and ready. I'd never hit anybody in my life, but just that second, I thought I could.

"I can handle this," Angel said from behind Max. "It's no big deal."

"Your sister's a retard," Max snarled at Peavine, only he couldn't really pronounce the word right. It came out *reee-tord*.

"You're trying to say 'retard,'" Peavine corrected, like he was talking to somebody who couldn't spell his own name. He gave Max the once-over, from his grubby tennis shoes to his lame band-logo T-shirt. "What you mean is 'intellectually disabled'—and you're stupid enough to think that's an insult. If you'd called her a gutless wonder like Max Selwin, now *that* woulda been rude."

Ruu-uude. Peavine's accent got stronger when he was mad. More kids crowded around, and a few laughed at what he said. I saw some people from our grade headed over too.

Max let go of his hurt arm and lurched toward Peavine, who pivoted smoothly out of his way.

"Stop it," Angel yelled. She started toward Peavine and Max, but I grabbed her. She dropped her book and tried to jerk out of my grip. "He's going to get hurt."

I held on tight. "Peavine's fine. He can take care of himself."

"No, he can't!"

Max swung his fist at Peavine, who just moved out of his way again—but the kid almost connected. Worry filled me up so fast, I didn't even realize I had let go of Angel until she was standing between Peavine and Max, both hands raised, palms out.

"You leave my brother alone!" she yelled.

Max made like he was going to walk off, then turned in a blink and planted his fist right in Angel's belly. She cried out and doubled over, hitting her knees. Before

Peavine could react, Max kicked Peavine's left-hand crutch out from under him.

I shouted and smacked the sides of my head with my hands. Peavine seemed to fall in slow motion. The smell of smoke burned my nose. My ears buzzed, then roared. Dizziness washed over me, and the world started changing and the day turned dark.

Happening again . . .

Not real . . .

But it *was* real.

A little boy crashed to the ground, right in the spot where Peavine had been standing. The boy was so small, so much thinner than Peavine, so much more breakable. A man loomed over him, fists swinging.

The world tilted and I ran forward, heart thudding. I threw myself at the man and hit at him before he could hurt the boy. He hit back. I expected pain and darkness, but his fists barely stung my chest and shoulders. I hit him some more, and people started yelling loud enough for me to hear it through the buzz in my ears, and the fire kept burning.

"Leave him alone!" I yelled. I couldn't breathe. Tears stung my eyes, then streamed down my face. "Don't touch him!"

My knuckles hit skin over and over, and the man let go of the little boy and covered his face with his arms and rolled into a ball, and hands grabbed me. Somebody shook me.

"Footer. Footer, stop!"

What was Ms. Malone doing at the Abrams farm?

What was I doing at the Abrams farm? I tried to pull away from the shaking, but I couldn't, and little by little the darkness and fire rattled right out of my head. Everything that wasn't real faded away, the day got bright and hot, and I was looking at my teacher instead of a man beating up a little boy. Max Selwin was curled up on the ground nearby, and some teachers were talking to him.

Across the street, the guy in the plaid shirt stood watching. He was drinking a Coke. I couldn't really see his face for the sweat in my eyes, but for some reason I thought he was laughing.

I glanced at Peavine, who had gotten to his feet. He had both metal crutches back in his grip. One looked a little dented. His right elbow was cut and bloody. Angel used the hem of her dress to dab at it, and she didn't look at me. Peavine nodded in my direction, like, *Thanks*. The hundred thousand million kids who had crowded around us, and the guy in plaid across the street, they just stared.

"I think you'd better come with me, Footer," Ms. Malone said.

She took my arm, and I let her lead me toward the office.

From the Notebook of Detective Peavine Jones

Interview of Rocky Davis, Eleven Days After the Fire

Location: Television Room in Footer's House

Mr. Davis: I'm only doing this to make Footer happy because she had a rotten day. You know that, right? None of us are actually suspects.

Footer: Thanks, Dad. [Hugs suspect.] Let's start with the fire. Where were you the night the Abrams farm burned?

Mr. Davis: At work.

Footer: Can anybody verify your alibi?

Mr. Davis: [Sighs] Will the night shift of the Bugtussle police force do?

Footer: I suppose. [Journalist chews the end of the pen she's carrying, even though she doesn't write anything during these interviews.]

Mr. Davis: Your mom always did that thing with the pen. [Suspect smiles.] All through school. Even back then she shone like a star for me, and I set out to be her sky.

Footer: Her sky? Dad, that's lame.

Mr. Davis: What does "lame" mean?

Footer: Dad can't be a real suspect, Peavine. He's too clueless. "Lame" means lame, Dad. You know, corny.

Mr. Davis: Adele called me her rock back then. Nothing corny about that. She said she wanted to be my flower. [Suspect closes his eyes for a second, then smiles.] Her sweet voice on the phone kept me going for my four years in the army, out in that endless desert. Not sure what I would have done if I hadn't had her love to guide me home. Folks wonder why I stick by her now that she's sick, but she's my wife, and she waited for me. The way I see it, it's my turn to wait for her.

Footer: That's sweet. [Journalist looks part happy, part sick.] Now, the night of the fire—

Mr. Davis: We made you together, didn't we, Footer? And I couldn't ask for a better daughter, even when you pretend I'm a murder and kidnapping and arson suspect. I was at work, kid. No way around it. Afraid I'm a dead end in your investigation.

Footer: [Journalist has mouth open, can't seem to respond. Detective takes over.]

Me: Mr. Davis, what do you think happened at the Abrams farm?

Mr. Davis: I honestly don't know, son, but I'm afraid those children died in the fire.

Me: Who shot Mr. Abrams?

Mr. Davis: I don't know the answer to that question either, but I figure it was somebody with a grudge.

Me: Why?

Mr. Davis: Because people don't usually shoot other people unless they're mad about something.

Me: But it could have been an accident, like with Ms. Davis and the snake—hey, what's your opinion on the events of today? That DCFS worker coming to see Footer, I mean?

Mr. Davis: That's probably not printable, Peavine. [Suspect frowns.] I'll take care of getting rid of those guns she's worried about before another day passes. I just hope Footer's smart enough not to tell that woman any of her wild ideas about serial killers and deadly walruses. You won't do that, right, Footer?

Footer: You're getting rid of our guns? No way, Dad!

Mr. Davis: I have to, honey. We have to face the possibility that life may never be just like it was before your mom got sick. For now we have to make changes to keep her safe—and us, too.

Footer: [Journalist looks very sad.]

She's been having a lot more problems since that fire. It's like she's more worried about Cissy and Doc than she is about us.

Mr. Davis: You're not exactly yourself either, beating up a boy on the playground, for God's sake. I know that kid jumped on Angel and Peavine, but still. Ms. Malone said it was like you were in another world. What were you thinking, Footer?

Footer: I—I want to see Mom.

Mr. Davis: I'll see what I can do, but I want you to stop making up all kinds of conspiracy theories about this fire and worrying yourself half to death.

Footer: Hey, I don't make up conspiracy theories. We really could have a rogue walrus on our hands.

Mr. Davis: To you, being funny is the same as being strong. I get that. But strong people don't smack younger kids on the playground. You need to keep a hold on yourself, and don't get too wrapped up in this detective-journalist thing you and Peavine are doing.

Footer: [Journalist gets the eating-lemons look and leaves the room. After three seconds, her bedroom door slams.]

Me: Um, okay.

Mr. Davis: Sometimes she reminds me so much of Adele, it scares me.

Me: Mr. Davis, will Footer get sick like her mom one day?

Mr. Davis: The doctors say there's a ten percent chance. But that means she's got a ninety percent chance of being just fine. [Suspect runs his hand over his face and looks tired.] If Footer gets sick too, I don't think I could stand it. I can't lose both of my girls, Peavine. I just can't.

To: crime-investigation/bureau-of-investigation@state.ms.gov
Cc: Peavine Jones
Bcc:
Subject: Creeps and Serial Killers
Attach: shoepic.jpg

Dear Mississippi Bureau of Investigation:

Your website is hard to figure out, and I couldn't really find a place to send information about current cases. The national FBI website had something about the Jackson office and a lot about civil rights—but no e-mail addresses either. So I'm using the general mailbox. Sorry if it's the wrong place.

My name is Fontana Davis, but most people call me Footer. I am eleven years old. I don't lie very much. It would be a lie if I said I never lied, so I'm not doing that, because you need to trust me.

I live near the Abrams farm in Bugtussle, where Cissy and Doc Abrams disappeared during a fire. My friends Peavine Jones and Angel Jones went with me to the farm to look around after the police guard left, because we wanted to figure out what happened. We didn't find anything important, but I kept thinking somebody was watching us. At first I thought I was going crazy (and so you don't get surprised, my mom has some problems like that, but she's in the hospital right now and I'm not, so I can't be too bad off, plus my dad's a veteran and a police officer, so that should count for something).

Angel took a lot of pictures, and when I downloaded them Sunday night, I found proof that maybe somebody was watching us. I attached the picture. It shows a shoe. I know you can't see if there's a leg in it, but it's pretty definitely a guy's shoe, and it had to get there some way. Captain Armstrong might have been wearing it. He's a veteran too, but he's not a police officer. I'm not turning him in or anything, because he's a really nice man, and he'd never murder anybody, but he does have shoes like that. Peavine and I checked the trail to the farm early this morning, and the shoe was gone. We didn't find any footprints, but we're not very good at looking for footprints.

We hope you will investigate this lead. Peavine wants to be a detective. I want to be a journalist. Never mind Angel, because she barely speaks normal English, and I think she wants to be an astronaut or a dragon rider, so she doesn't count. All three of us want to help, though.

Thank you very much,

Footer Davis
footGurrrl@mmail.com
Sent from my iPhone

From the Notebook of Detective Peavine Jones

Interview of Regina Jones, Eleven Days After the Fire

Location: Television Room in Footer's House

Mom: Don't you think it's awfully close to bedtime to start a criminal interview?

Footer: We're interviewing suspects in the Abrams fire, not criminals.

Mom: Then this will be fast, because I was at a church potluck with my kids when that fire was set. About forty people saw us.

Footer: [Journalist frowns. She's still pretty, though.] You have a point. What's for dinner tomorrow? Dad said you were cooking for us.

Mom: I'll have to see what you've got here, but I'll go to the store first, so no worries. I'll make sure it doesn't have any flies in it, or snake guts. That a deal?

Footer: No walrus meat either.

Mom: [Suspect raises right hand.] Word

of honor. I was thinking more like baked chicken.

Footer: What do people do after they win the lottery?

Mom: Well, I didn't win a gigantic jackpot, so I just paid off our debt, set up some savings and investments, stopped working for the county, and took a part-time job doing the accounting for my church.

Footer: You never have problems like my mom, do you?

Mom: Everybody has problems, Footer. Remember when you first met Peavine, back when you two were in kindergarten—before he got strong enough to really use his forearm crutches?

Footer: Sort of.

Mom: That first day at school, he had so much trouble just walking up the front steps, and he cried, and you were the only one who didn't laugh at him. You were the only one who helped him. [suspect looks sad, and I wish she wouldn't talk about that stuff.] I was a mess all that day, to be honest. And that night, and all the next week. Every surgery Peavine's had to help him stand up straight and walk better, the day the doctor told me Angel might have some social and learning problems, the night I came home and found their father gone—no family is perfect, and I'm sure not, myself. Trust me, I've been a mess lots of times.

Footer: But you haven't had to go to that hospital in Memphis.

Mom: No, I haven't. [suspect looks sad again. I really hate it when she looks sad.] You and your dad and mom have always been there for us, though. You've never let Peavine or Angel down, and your parents were right there with me when I've had to go through my big problems. So, if I ever did have to go to that hospital in Memphis, I bet you and your dad would help Peavine and Angel while I was gone—and your mom would help, too, if she was feeling up to it.

Footer: Of course we would.

Mom: [Suspect hugs journalist.] Okay, now, seriously. It's time for bed, both of you. Peavine, find your sister and get your things.

Extra note: I bet older detectives do not have bedtimes or have to put up with people hugging their suspects and journalists.

CHAPTER 8

Twelve Days After the Fire

"Captain Armstrong took all Dad's guns away last night. He's going to keep them at his house."

Mom didn't say anything.

"When he came over," I told her, "he had on black running shoes. They look like this shoe in a picture Peavine and I took at the crime scene."

Mom still didn't say anything.

"Do you think Captain Armstrong could be an actual suspect?" I stared at Mom, who wasn't moving, and who wasn't really looking at me. "Not a practice one, like you and Dad. Since he used to be a soldier and all, maybe he's shot people before?"

Nothing from Mom.

"I mean, he could have had one of his flashbacks. Some people in town think that. There are rumors that maybe he was over there that night, or running past the farm for some reason and thought Mr. Abrams was an enemy. It could happen, right?"

"Enemy," Mom muttered, and I jumped. I leaned toward her, hoping she'd keep talking, but she went right back to staring at nothing.

"I don't think he did it," I said. "Captain Armstrong wouldn't kill anybody now, would he, Mom?"

Nothing.

Alone with Mom in a visitor's room at the hospital psychiatric unit, I looked down at my scratched knuckles. I couldn't believe I beat up a little kid yesterday. Did I really hit Max Selwin over and over? I kinda remembered doing it, but kinda not, too. Mostly I remembered smelling fire and seeing darkness and then seeing the creep in the plaid shirt watching from across the street.

He had been smiling.

The suspicious stranger.

Captain Armstrong and the creep were more likely to have had something to do with the Abrams crimes than my mom. I felt sure of that.

Outside the visitor's-room door, Dad and one of the nurses talked in low voices. I wondered if they were discussing Mom or me. Did this place have a unit for kids? I hoped it didn't.

Mom shifted in her rolling recliner, making her hospital blanket rustle. I glanced up at her, hating the way her face just hung on her bones, not moving. I double-hated knowing she couldn't even walk, because her thoughts were moving so fast, she couldn't pay attention to anything for long, not even her feet.

The room we were in was about the size of Ms. Malone's classroom at school. It was painted all whites and yellows with pictures of flowers and words stenciled around like BELIEVE and HOPE and I AM MORE THAN MY ILLNESS. It was bright and cheerful and everything smelled like coconut air freshener, but my mother looked like a zombie.

"I think I have a brain tumor," I told Mom.

No reaction.

I tried again. "The lady from Children and Family Services, her names is Stephanie Bridges. She's the one who made Dad get rid of his guns. I guess she was afraid you'd shoot me instead of a snake."

Mom stayed still in her chair. Her mouth dropped wide, but not like she was surprised. More like she was about to snore with her eyes open.

"Are you awake?" I muttered.

"I'm awake," she said, slurring the words. "Guns. Sorry, my fault."

It was her fault, so I didn't tell her it wasn't.

"Shotguns and rifles are dangerous," she added. "Maybe it's for the best." Then she mumbled for a while, not saying anything that made sense. The medications did that to her sometimes. She told me that was one of the reasons she didn't like taking them.

I'd rather be crazy than stupid, Fontana.

Not me.

If somebody gave me pills to chase away crazy, I'd take every one of them, just like I was supposed to.

"I think I'm losing my mind," I whispered.

Mom sat up a little straighter, and the wheels on her rolling recliner creaked. "You're fine, honey."

"I'm not fine." Flutters started in my belly, and I couldn't look at her. The closest picture to me had roses and daisies mixed together, and it didn't look normal, all that red in the white and yellow. "I keep seeing things."

"If you were losing your mind, you'd hear things, not see things," Mom said. "What are you seeing?"

My eyes went from roses and daisies to the shadow of Dad outside the visiting-room door. "The fire. Cissy Abrams."

"Sshhh. Hush now." Mom's face tightened and now she sat as straight as any normal person. "You slept through all of that, remember?"

I picked at the cut knuckles on my right hand, making them bleed. "What if I didn't?"

Mom kept blinking, like she wanted to nod off but was too scared to do it.

"When did you lose your barrette?" I asked her.

She blinked faster. "We don't need to waste time

talking about barrettes. That's over and done."

My heart did a big plummet, right down in the fluttery flitters. It wasn't over and done. Nothing felt over and done. "It's not wasting time. Mom, if you were there during the fire, if I was there, we can't just pretend it away."

Her hands twitched under her white blanket. "I want you to feed the mice, Footer. Can you do that for me? Feed the mice in the basement, so they don't die like my squirrel."

"What are you talking about? Mom—"

"Rifles and shotguns are too dangerous for little girls, even if we have a right to them." Mom blinked and blinked and blinked. "Our country was founded on the Bill of Rights. Did you know that? This is a great country—"

I stared at her, not hearing her anymore because a high whine had started in my ears.

Rifles and shotguns are too dangerous for little girls.

The whine got louder, until it buzzed.

No. Not now. Not here.

But I couldn't help blinking like Mom did, too fast, over and over, because it was happening again. The world was changing. Hallucination. Flashback. Mice and dead squirrels. Help me.

I dug my fingers into the chair arms and the room turned into fire, and—

Cissy Abrams stands in front of me, covered in moonlight. . . .

She holds out her arms. . . .

A shotgun appears in her hands. . . .

Dark flecks rain down. . . .

Mom appears beside Cissy. . . .

She puts her hands on the shotgun. . . .

"Hurry," she says. . . .

They look at me. . . .

I start to fall. . . .

"My country, 'tis of theeeee," a voice sang so loud, it broke the night around me. I threw out my arms to keep from hitting the ground, and my fingers brushed soft blanket.

My eyes focused on Mom. Mom in her hospital rolling chair, without a shotgun or any fire burning around her.

"Mom!" My heart thumped as I gripped the blanket on top of her. "I saw—I thought I saw you and Cissy and—"

Mom giggled and stuck out one of her hands. "I have a piano in my wrist, see?" She sang again, louder than ever, *"Sweet land of liiiii-berty, of thee I sing!"*

I fixed my gaze on her arm, and tears ran down my cheeks. Everything inside me hurt, but I tried again anyway. "Mom, I thought I saw you at the fire. Just now. It happened again. Talk to me, Mom, please?"

"Land where my faaaaa-thers died, land of the piiiiiil-grim's pride!" Mom didn't even look at me as she sang, only now it was more like yelling.

Dad and the nurse came in and tried to talk to Mom, but she babbled about feeding mice and wearing barrettes, then fell asleep before they could get very far.

"Sorry," the nurse told me as I wiped the tears off my face. "We're still a little early in getting her calmed down. If you come back next week—"

"Piano," Mom mumbled, then moved her fingers on her arm like she was playing the piano and went back to snoring.

I felt sick.

Dad shook his head as the nurse pushed Mom out of the visiting room and back toward the big metal double doors that led into the psychiatric unit. As the nurse punched in a code, Dad ran his fingers through his brown curls. My brain registered that his hair always stayed flat on top, like he had just pulled off his police-uniform hat. He wasn't wearing his uniform because we were visiting this hospital. He had on jeans and a black button-up shirt, and I could see the round outline of a chewing-tobacco tin in his back pocket.

The doors to the locked psychiatric unit swung open with a whoosh. I got a strong blast of alcohol mixed with body odor and old poop and something like spinach. The nurse pushed my mother through and the doors swung shut, trapping Mom in all that disgusting stink, and I wanted to cry all over again. I couldn't keep crying, though. If I did, Dad would never bring me back here, and I'd have to wait weeks to see Mom again.

Dad's big hand rested on my shoulder. "Want to grab a hot dog from Chicago Eats, Footer?"

I tried to nod, but my neck felt too stiff. I probably did have a brain tumor, and it was gigantic and weighed three hundred pounds, and it would kill me by tomorrow. Since I'd probably be dead before sunrise, I should eat as many hot dogs as I could.

"Cheese," Dad added as we walked out of the little room with pictures of roses and daisies. "And some chili. Maybe onions and kraut. Onions and kraut are vegetables."

"Kraut's not a real vegetable, is it?" I asked, trying to make myself focus on hot dogs ruined by pickled cabbage, but thinking about brain tumors and mice and barrettes and shotguns.

The jelly was gone. When I looked in the pantry, we were out of peanut butter and bread, too. And a bunch of other stuff, like my fruit drinks and the cookies I always took in my lunch.

Mice in the basement, Mom?

More like rhinoceros rats.

Except it wasn't rats or mice, it was probably me. Jeez. Did I eat *that* much when I walked in my sleep

Sunday night? Well, Monday too. Still, it was hard to believe I could take out an entire jar of jelly without throwing up grape for days.

I burped chili hot dog, then yelled, "Dad, we need to go to the store."

"Why?" he asked from the living room.

"Because we're out of everything."

"There was half a jar of peanut butter and a whole loaf of bread when I made your lunch yesterday." I heard the creak of his chair as he got up to come see what I was talking about.

"You must have thrown it away by mistake, then, because it's gone now."

Mom's mice ate it. Yeah. Great big huge hallucination mice. My lips twitched. Smiling about anything right now seemed wrong, but I couldn't help it. I kept seeing dinosaur mice with purple, jelly-smeared whiskers.

"Huh." Dad came into the kitchen, gazed into the pantry, scratched his head, and closed the door.

The phone on the counter rang, and I picked it up, figuring it was Peavine. "Hello?"

Silence answered me. I pulled the phone away from my ear and read the display. It said OUT OF AREA.

"Hello?" I said again, ramping up my annoyed tone and wondering if it was a stupid telemarketer.

"May I speak to Adele Davis, please?" a woman asked, her words a little slurred.

"She's not here right now. May I take a message?"

"No. That's okay. Thanks." The woman hung up.

I punched the receiver off and dropped it back in its cradle, wondering who the woman was. Probably somebody from one of Mom's online support groups for bipolar disorder. She knew a lot of people that way.

"It's okay, Footer," Dad said. "We'll run to the store tomorrow afternoon. Maybe you could help me make a list?"

I leaned against him as he opened a drawer and pulled out a pad. "Just get everything we like. And some ice cream."

Fish sticks, Dad wrote, instead of ice cream.

"Are there walruses in fish sticks?"

"Uh, no. Pretty sure not." He glanced down at me and grinned, which made me feel better about all of life, at least for a second.

"Okay." I covered my mouth and burped chili hot dog again. "But could we do chicken nuggets instead, just for a little while? Chicken nuggets definitely do not have walrus meat."

"Sometimes I worry about you, Footer." Dad sounded tickled more than worried as he wrote *ice cream*.

"Sometimes I worry about me too, Dad."

He patted my head, then sent me to get ready for bed. I let him tuck me in, then waited until he turned his light off. Then I pushed my door until it was almost closed, so the light from my lamp wouldn't wake him. After that I sat at my desk because I didn't want to get into bed, because if I got into bed and shut my eyes, what if I had more hallucinations?

The thought made my heart beat funny, and I didn't like it. After a minute or so, I opened my computer and read about hallucinations and bipolar disorder. I read page after page on the two big symptoms of Mom's illness, mania and depression. Sometimes I could match myself to the mania stuff, like, *talking very fast* and *jumping from one idea to another* and *being easily distracted.* I could even go for *being restless* and *having trouble sleeping*.

Weird.

Didn't everybody have times when they talked fast and thought fast and got distracted? Was I the only person in the world who got bored and fidgety in class, or sometimes when I didn't have things to do in the afternoon? And sleeping. It wasn't always a problem.

Besides, I didn't think I had *an unrealistic belief in one's abilities*. *Spending sprees* were out, since I didn't have any money, and *impulsive business investments* . . . Yeah. Maybe someday, but not now. None of the depression symptoms seemed to fit me either, except maybe the *restless and irritable* part, and the *change in eating and sleeping habits*.

And, of course, I didn't think I had a piano in my wrist.

If I wasn't getting totally sick like Mom, and I wasn't really hallucinating, then everything I saw was probably a flashback.

A sudden, usually powerful, re-experiencing of a past experience or elements of a past experience. . . .

I clicked off the mental-health websites and closed my eyes. Flashbacks. Like maybe I was there that night after all. I didn't want that to be real, but I didn't want to be having hallucinations, either. And if all of that at the Abrams farm was one giant awful flashback, then . . .

My fingers selected a file and clicked the mouse, even though I didn't really want them to. I sat there staring at my list and listening to myself breathe and feeling my heart race, then stop, race, then stop.

Then I got busy with strikeout.

1. Old Mr. Abrams got shot, ~~and nobody knows who shot him.~~ ***MOM OR CISSY SHOT HIM WITH A SHOTGUN. WHY?***
2. The Abrams farm got burned to the ground, ~~and nobody knows who set the fire.~~ ***MOM OR CISSY SET THE FIRE. WHY?***
3. Cissy and Doc might be dead or alive, and nobody knows where they are.
4. Mom ~~might have been~~ ***WAS*** there.
5. I ~~might have been~~ ***WAS*** there.
6. Somebody might have been watching us while we searched. ***THE SOMEBODY HAD SHOES***

JUST LIKE CAPTAIN ARMSTRONG.

7. I ~~might be~~ ***PROBABLY AM*** crazy.

When I finished, I saved it under REALLY PROBABLY CRAZY LIST. Then I closed the file, shut the laptop, and put my head down on its warm lid. When people solved mysteries on TV, they didn't keep getting bigger questions and worse stuff to worry about, did they?

I was pretty sure I had some answers now.

The problem was, I didn't want any of them.

Critical Thinking: Serial Killers Don't Wear Plaid

Footer Davis
5th Period
Ms. Perry

I. Hypothesis

Serial killers don't wear plaid shirts. Is this always true, sometimes true, partly true, or false?

II. Evidence Collected

I looked at all the pictures in a dictionary of serial killers, then searched 1,354 photos online. A few serial killers might have been wearing plaid, but I couldn't tell for sure. Serial killers seem to prefer button-ups with T-shirts underneath, or jail jumpsuits, unless they are Russian. Russian serial killers wear really freaky-looking stuff, even in jail. Most serial killers have stupid nicknames people shouldn't give them, like Black Angel and Deathmaker and the Giggling Granny. Those names make them sound like heroes or comic-book characters, not something scary and evil. They also have bad hairdos, and some have moustaches that look like they belong on clowns. One serial killer dressed up like a clown. If

Serial killer dressed as a clown. This is a good reason not to like clowns.

you type in "serial killer" and search for it, you get about 164 million hits. If you type in "God," you get more than a billion hits. So at least the world hasn't gone "totally BLEEPing insane" like my neighbor Captain Armstrong says.

III. What I Learned from This Report

1. Russian serial killers are stranger and uglier than walruses, and God is still more popular than maniacs.
2. My hypothesis that serial killers don't wear plaid is sometimes or always true.
3. The guy watching the school from across the street at the store is probably a creep, not a serial killer, because he wears plaid shirts.

PLEASE SEE ME AFTER CLASS.

CHAPTER 9

Thirteen Days After the Fire

If I had a brain tumor, it was growing very slowly, because I was still alive and having to go to school. That sucked. Not the being-alive part but the school part. I wasn't much in the mood for school. I never was when Mom had to be away.

"I was supposed to see Ms. Perry yesterday after class, but I didn't go," I admitted to Peavine on Thursday as we sat behind the scraggly bushes next to the school, doing surveillance on the creep at the convenience store. He was back again, wearing plaid and eating his lunch and staring at kids out at recess. "Think she'll send me to the office?"

"She might. You know she's strict." Branches and leaves covered most of Peavine's face, but when he glanced at me I could see the bright blue of his eyes through the brush. "What'd you do to tick her off this time?"

"She didn't like the paper I wrote." The guy across the street chomped on his hot dog. He ate a hot dog every day. I wondered if he put the same stuff on it. That would be boring, and probably more like a serial killer than a creep, since serial killers liked everything the same.

Peavine sighed. "She never likes your papers, Footer, but it's nothing personal. She hates my stuff too."

"You always write about worms and fishing and baseball." I batted at the branch closest to my face, then snapped it so I could see better, then I didn't want to see better, because I was feeling guilty and I'd been feeling guilty for days and just couldn't stand it anymore. "I think Angel found my mother's barrette at the Abrams farm. I tried to ask Mom about it when I visited Wednesday, but she just talked about mice in the basement and got all weird about having a piano in her wrist and sang really loud." I cleared my throat and made myself look in his general direction, even though I saw mostly bush instead of his face. "I'm sorry I didn't say anything before."

"I didn't want to ask you about the barrette, but I've been worried about it," Peavine admitted. His blue eyes seemed twice as big as usual, and he was whispering, even though nobody was close to us. There were hundreds of kids out messing around everywhere, but here between the bushes and a brick wall, it seemed like we were alone in the universe. My eyes drifted to a rock on the ground, and I thought about Dad saying Mom was his star, but Mom calling Dad a rock and wanting to be his flower. Peavine was my strong, sturdy rock, right down here on the ground where I needed him. I didn't know how he saw me. I hoped I was his rock, or maybe his flower beside the rock.

"I've been worried too," I whispered back. My throat felt a little dry. I wanted to tell him I didn't think the barrette wasn't any big deal, but I couldn't look him straight in those sweet blue eyes and lie, and besides, I didn't want to start feeling guilty all over again. "I guess Mom lost the barrette."

Peavine dug into the dirt with one hand, scooting little piles of dust forward, toward the bush's gnarled trunk. "Do you think your mom was at the Abrams farm the night of the fire?"

My stomach twisted up, but I made myself breathe in and out, really slow like it said to on this YouTube video I watched on my phone last night. It was about stopping flashbacks and relaxation and "centering," whatever that meant. The breathing helped enough to let me talk.

"Maybe she was there," I said. Then before I could chicken out, I added, "Maybe I was there too."

So much for breathing. My whole chest hurt like a walrus might be sitting on me with its giant walrus butt right on my ribs. Had I said that? Had I really, really just told Peavine I thought I was at the Abrams farm the night of the fire?

I was going to die of not breathing and thinking about walrus butts.

As I saw twinkly spots and tried not to think about walruses and opened my mouth to breathe, Peavine knocked his dust pile over.

"Seriously? You think you were at the farm, Footer? You making that up?"

I shook my head and made myself breathe, breathe, breathe. No walruses. No walrus butts. None. Absolutely no thinking about walrus butts.

"I've been seeing things," I told Peavine when I could talk. "You know, like Mom does? Hallucinations. Only, I don't think they're really hallucinations. I read about those, and other stuff, and I think I'm having flashbacks. I think maybe I'm remembering stuff, but when I try to really think about it, it disappears and I just feel crazy. It's like I can't look at what's right in front of me."

Or right beside you, my mind whispered. *In the dark, waiting to pounce. . . .*

I shook my head to make that stupid brain-voice shut its mouth. Would Peavine believe me about being at the Abrams farm the night of the fire? Did I even believe myself? I doubled both hands into fists and pressed them into the warm dirt, breathing the hot air and staring mostly at the leaves right in front of my nose. A suspicious stranger might have burned down the farm. Or a creep. Or Captain Armstrong. I was crazy. I had to be.

Peavine snapped a few branches so he could look at me better. "You're not crazy, Footer," he said, and he sounded so certain, he almost made me believe it. "Quit worrying so much. Whatever's going on, you and me, we'll figure it out together, okay?"

The way he was looking at me, so sure and so sweet and so completely Peavine, I wanted to kiss him.

So I kissed him.

I didn't want to talk about the barrette or the fire anymore, and Peavine was always so nice to me, and I wanted to know how it felt to put my lips on a real boy's lips instead of my own arm pretending, before I got locked up in a hospital like Mom for the rest of my life and never got to kiss anyone.

I had pretended to kiss Peavine before, and some other boys, but mostly Peavine. This real kiss lasted two seconds, and it was nothing like pretending. He tasted like salt and the barbecue potato chips he always ate at lunch, and there was a leaf right at the corner of our mouths, and a branch scratched my ear when I did it.

Peavine kept his eyes open. I know, because mine were open too. His eyes got a lot bigger as I pulled back, and he just stared at me for a second. The right side of his mouth twitched, like he wanted to grin but he was too freaked out. Finally, he said, "Okay," and breathed a few times.

"Okay?" I wasn't breathing at all. "That's it?"

"I—uh, no, I—did you mean to do that?"

"Yeah."

"Okay." He grinned with both sides of his mouth.

I grinned back, then realized my heart was beating really, really fast. "Do you think I'm a rock or a flower?"

"What?"

"A flower and a rock, like my mom said about her and dad when they first met, remember?"

Peavine still looked totally blank.

"A flower." I got all hot in the face and started to sweat while he thought about it. "Like clover. All delicate and pretty and stuff. Or a rock. Like plain, strong granite. Which am I?"

"Is there a right answer to this?" When I didn't say anything, he asked, "Can I think about it?"

My heart wouldn't quit racing, even though he didn't choose. Honest, I didn't even know which I wanted him to pick. So I just said, "Okay." And then, "What do you think he's really doing, that creep over there?"

My voice shook when I asked the question, and I wondered if Peavine would tease me or ask me the difference between a rock and a flower, or make us talk about why I kissed him. I really didn't want to talk about it, even though I thought I might want to kiss him again someday.

For a few more seconds Peavine just sat there watching as the guy in the sleeveless plaid shirt finished his hot dog and threw away his trash. "I think the guy's casing the playground," he finally answered.

I was so relieved, I almost busted out laughing, even though I *would* have seemed crazy if I've done that. "Why is he so interested in our recess?"

Peavine shrugged, making the bush branches rustle. "Because he's a creep, like you said."

The man did seem to be scanning the playground. He kept moving his head back and forth, slow, like he was searching for something, staying mostly on our side.

I felt silly, and almost dizzy, maybe from spilling all my secrets and not having to feel like a jerk anymore, or maybe from kissing Peavine. The world turned faster than it was supposed to, and my ears buzzed, and I still wanted to laugh.

"You think he could be looking for us?" I asked Peavine.

"What would he want us for?"

"No idea." I choked back a giggle. "But let's see what he does."

I stood up fast, before Peavine could talk me out of it.

"Footer!" Peavine jumped up too, and a bunch of kids throwing a football nearby stopped to look at us.

The guy across the street saw us too, and he got real still. His eyes locked on mine, and I was pretty sure his eyebrows went up. My heart thumped and thumped, and all of a sudden I didn't feel like laughing anymore. I started smelling smoke.

Oh, no.

The front part of my brain tried to shove away any thought of fire before I flipped out on the playground again and got myself kicked out of school or sent to a hospital or locked in a room with Stephanie Bridges. The back part of my brain started screaming. Red lights stabbed into my eyes, blinking and swirling, and a loud noise made me flinch.

"It's the police," Peavine said from what seemed like a quadrillion miles away from me. He sounded awed.

How was he seeing my hallucinations? That wasn't even possible. He couldn't—

Oh.

The police. The red lights, the noise—a police car had pulled into the parking lot across the street from the school, and two uniformed officers I didn't know got out. Both of them walked toward the creep in plaid, who raised his hands like he was saying, *Easy now*, or *I got no gun*, or *I'm a nice guy—don't arrest me*.

The officers stopped in front of the guy. Both of them had short hair. They were wearing sunglasses, and their arms were crossed. If I were the creep, I'd be nervous, because they really didn't look friendly.

"Footer," somebody said, and I realized Ms. Malone had snuck up beside the bushes while we watched all the action across the road. Her tone didn't sound friendly either. She had on sunglasses, and her arms were crossed just like the police's were.

I didn't smell any more smoke, and I didn't feel the least little bit silly. I didn't even feel like kissing Peavine again, for the moment.

"Ms. Perry needs to see you," Ms. Malone said. "Now. And after that, you and I, we need to talk."

From the Notebook of Detective Peavine Jones

Interview of Nadine Perry, Twelve Days After the Fire

Location: Ms. Perry's Fifth-Grade Classroom

This is proof that I am brave enough to be a detective.

Me: Thank you for agreeing to do this interview about the fire.

Ms. Perry: Young man, I am only doing this because Ms. Malone asked me to keep you busy while Fontana Davis serves her detention, since she has to ride home with you and your mother.

Me: She likes to be called Footer.

Ms. Perry: That is a ridiculous nickname.

Me: Um, yes, ma'am. Sorry.

Ms. Perry: I have no problem with you, Mr. Jones. You take your work seriously, and you try to be a decent influence on your sister.

Me: Um, thank you, ma'am. About the fire, can you tell me where you were the night the Abrams farm burned?

Ms. Perry: I was out to a nice dinner with Mr. Drake.

Me: The librarian?

Ms. Perry: [Says nothing. Looks pretty scary.]

Me: Um, okay. So, do you have any thoughts about what might have happened to Cissy and Doc Abrams?

Ms. Perry: They died in that fire, of course. No doubt Fontana has filled you full of silly notions about them surviving. She has more intelligence than any child needs, but she squanders her potential. How she can bring any topic back around to walruses and serial killers—it beggars the imagination. Look at her writing her sentences. I'm positive she's thinking about marine mammals and murderers instead of how to treat her schoolwork with more seriousness.

Me: Yes, ma'am. I mean, no, ma'am. I'm sure Footer is taking this very seriously.

Ms. Perry: I think she's the biggest challenge I've faced in thirty-three years of teaching social studies. I fear she's headed down the same path as her mother.

Me: [Detective is silent. Are detectives always supposed to know what to say?]

Ms. Perry: Mr. Jones, your friend attacked a younger boy on the playground. I know you all say the other boy started it, but I think both Fontana and the boy should have been suspended. Without discipline and structure, Fontana will never learn to face life on life's terms. She'll wind up just like her mother, living more in fantasy than reality.

Me: [Detective remains silent.]

Ms. Perry: For example, her latest insistence that a "creep" has been watching the school's lunch recess gave me no choice but to call the authorities. No doubt some law-abiding citizen will be harassed and questioned because a little girl read too much about serial killers and scared herself. She has been much worse since that terrible fire, and I understand that her mother has been hospitalized again. It would not surprise me at all to learn that Adele Davis has to stay in the hospital a very long time. Maybe that's what needs to happen.

Me: Um, about the fire again. There are other suspects. Like the creep, or Captain Armstrong. What do you think about—

Ms. Perry: I understand that Fontana's father took her to see her mother. [Suspect shakes her head.] I think that's too much stress for Fontana. I'm glad that DCFS authorities have gotten involved. Maybe they can bring some order in Fontana's life before it's too late for her.

Me: Thank you for your time, Ms. Perry.

Reflections on Respect and Following Instructions

Footer Davis
Lunch Recess Detention
Ms. Perry
Page 10 of 10

90. I will treat my teachers with respect and follow instructions.
91. I will treat my teachers with respect and follow instructions.
92. I will treat my teachers with respect and follow instructions.
93. I will treat my teachers with respect and follow instructions.
94. I will treat my teachers with respect and follow instructions.
95. I will treat my teachers with respect and follow instructions.
96. I will treat my teachers with respect and follow instructions.
97. I will treat my teachers with respect and follow instructions.
98. I will treat my teachers with respect and follow instructions.
99. I will treat my teachers with respect and follow instructions, unless the instructions involve walruses.
100. I will treat my teachers with respect and follow instructions, unless the instructions involve walruses (or serial killers).

CHAPTER 10

Still Thirteen Days After the Fire

Captain Armstrong: Who are you, and why is Footer in your car?
Stephanie Bridges: I'm Stephanie Bridges. I'm with DCFS, and I offered to drive her home because Ms. Jones needed to meet with Angel's teacher and I have to do a home visit.
Captain Armstrong: You got some ID?
Stephanie Bridges: This is my name tag. Here, take a look.
Captain Armstrong: Lady, this world has gone totally [censored] insane. Anyone can have that kind of crap made. I want to see something official.
Stephanie Bridges: All right. Let me get my

wallet. Here we go. My official identification card.

Captain Armstrong: Guess you're legit. You okay in there, kid?

Me: Yes, sir.

Captain Armstrong: I'll let your father know she's here and that I checked her out.

Me: Thanks, Captain Armstrong.

Captain Armstrong: You know, Ms. Bridges, these people have enough problems without you making everything worse.

"You with me there, Footer?"

I wound my way back from the numb conversation snapshots and made myself look at how the afternoon sunlight twinkled off Stephanie Bridges's blond hair as she got out of her car in my driveway. Keeping her eyes on Captain Armstrong as he ambled back up the street, she came around and opened my door for me, since she had me child-locked inside.

As I climbed out, she asked, "Is that man okay?"

My heart bounced against my ribs because she seemed genuinely worried, which worried me and made me hate her a little less and made me hate her a little more. "He's a veteran like my dad," I told her. My gaze drifted to Captain Armstrong as he got to his own yard, and I couldn't help smiling. He looked all big and scary, but he was so nice to me, and to everybody. So he had a pair of black serial-killer stalker-creep tennis shoes. That didn't make him guilty.

Did it?

"He put his number in my phone so I can call him whenever I want," I added so Stephanie Bridges would understand how he helped me and anybody who needed him. "He's great, so you just leave him alone. I don't want him disappearing like Dad's guns."

She leaned against her purple car and frowned at me as I sat down on one of Mom's stone landscape walls. "I can tell you're angry with me. It's because of the guns, right?"

"Captain Armstrong even took my BB gun, and Dad says we can't go get it right now." I folded my arms and tried to look as mean as the police who questioned the guy in plaid. "Dad and I won't be able to go shooting this weekend, Stephanie Bridges. Are you happy?"

She sighed. "You can call me Steph. That'll be easier than saying my whole name every time you talk—and surely you and your dad can find safer activities than target shooting?"

"Like what, soccer? I broke my arm playing soccer two years ago." How was I supposed to call her Steph? She was older than me. People older than me were Mr. or Ms. Besides, I didn't like her enough to call her Steph.

"Dad can't play soccer with me because he has bad knees," I went on, not having to work at looking mad. "I like football, but I can't play it. I suck at baseball, I've never gotten a basketball through a hoop in my life, ever, and I hate NASCAR. That pretty much leaves target shooting as stuff I can do with a dad in Mississippi, and you took that away. Thanks. Why do you hate guns so much, anyway?"

She looked at the ground near my feet. "I—well. It's not that I hate them, exactly. It's just, even when I was just a student learning to be a social worker I saw guns do a lot of bad things."

"Bad people do bad things," I said. "Not guns."

"Guns make it a lot easier for bad people to be bad."

I knew I wasn't going to win this argument, so I quit trying, which made her look worried.

"You could go hiking, maybe?" she asked. "Or canoeing?"

"I'm clumsy when I'm learning new stuff, and you'll put me in foster care if I turn up with a bruise."

Stephanie Bridges—Steph?—said, "So, you're scared I'll take you away from your mom and dad."

I unfolded my arms. "Well, yeah. Isn't that what you people do?"

"Sometimes." She seemed to shrink into the car. "We have some very good foster parents, but that's never our first choice. Usually we just help families who are having problems."

"By taking away BB guns?"

"I'm sorry about that."

"Don't lie to me." I got off the wall and stalked toward the front door. "Lying brings bad luck, and I hate it when people lie to me."

"Okay, I'm not sorry." Stephanie Bridges hurried after me, her voice getting closer with each word. "My very first case with DCFS, the father shot the mother right after I left from a visit. Guns make me nervous. All guns."

I fished my key out of my pocket, crammed it in the lock, then shoved open the front door. "That's stupid. He was a bad man. It wasn't the gun's fault."

"You're entitled to your opinion." She followed me into the house.

"Your opinion is the only one that counts."

"It counts some, but your father's opinion counts more. He chose to give the guns to your neighbor rather than take any chances with your safety."

I went all the way to the kitchen before I stopped and turned on her again, glaring up into her wide brown eyes. "So what are we supposed to do about the next poisonous snake? Hack it to bits with a rake or something? That'll be *soooo* much safer."

She looked miserable, but she didn't say anything.

I walked away from her and headed for my afternoon snack.

"Why did you write a paper about serial killers, Footer?" she asked as I opened the pantry, her words so quiet, I barely heard her.

I wanted to bang my head on the top shelf, I really did. I also wanted her to finish her inspection and go away. "Why do I always have to answer questions? Why don't you answer a few, like what's the real color of your hair?"

"It's brown, lighter than my eyes, kind of like a field mouse," she said without any hesitation at all. "I never liked it."

Great. Now I felt like a butthead. I really needed not to be mean to Stephanie Bridges. And where were my drinks? My brownies? I pawed through the pantry's few boxes and cans of soup. Dad and I bought a bunch of stuff at the store yesterday. Where was it? No way I sleep-ate *that* much in a single night.

Did I?

"Do you like being blond?" I mumbled, thinking more about the food that had gone into hiding than what I was saying.

"Blond isn't bad. I may try redhead next. You and your mom have beautiful hair."

I stopped pawing and turned around to face her. "You talked to Mom?"

"I tried." She gave me a rueful smile. "She kept grabbing my hands and telling me she had a piano."

"The one in her wrist." My stomach felt funny. "Yeah. I got to hear about that too."

"She asked me to feed the mice in the basement."

"Me too."

Stephanie Bridges didn't seem to know what to say to any of that, and I didn't either. When Mom got sick, she talked out of her head, but sometimes she tried to tell me stuff that was important to her. The words couldn't swim through her brain fog, and I wasn't always smart enough to put the meaning together. I wished that I could. Maybe if I could understand what her crazy talk meant to her, I could help her get better faster. Mice and pianos—I just had no idea.

Stephanie Bridges came toward me, close enough to make me back up into the pantry. "Did I upset you just now, talking about your mom?"

Yes. I hate talking about Mom being sick, especially to people I don't know.

But I didn't know her well enough, so out loud I said, "No. I was just trying to figure out the mice and the piano thing. Usually Mom's obsessed with snakes. It might all mean something, or it might not."

"Like you and your serial killers?"

I rolled my eyes better than Peavine ever thought about doing. "Ms. Perry hates me. I wrote about serial killers just to freak her out because she makes me mad, and you can't tell teachers off any other way."

This made Stephanie Bridges go quiet for a minute. Finally, she came out with "Fair enough."

"And don't go investigating Ms. Perry or anything," I

said as I edged out of the pantry. "She's not abusive. She's just a—well, a not-nice person most of the time."

"Do you ever think about hurting yourself or other people?"

"No." I slammed the pantry door behind me. "You creep me out when you ask stuff like that."

"Stuff about how you feel?"

"No, stuff like the doctors ask my mother. I'm not mentally ill, even if Ms. Perry would get a kick out of me going nuts."

"I can see why those questions would make you angry, then," Steph said. "Thanks for telling me."

Steph. Yeah, I was giving up.

"I'm sorry," Steph said. "I won't ask that kind of stuff anymore, if you'll promise to tell me if you ever do start having thoughts like that."

"Fine. I promise. And for the record, I don't lie very much."

"Y'all don't have much food, do you?"

No, because we have dinosaur mice in the basement. That, or I've been hallucinating, sleepwalking, and sleep-eating. Yay? "We're going to the store soon." That wasn't a lie, because we'd have to make a run to restock. Dad was going to kill me—unless he was sleep-eating too.

"Want to see the rest of the house?" I walked out of the kitchen, into the living room. My eyes darted all around, making sure I didn't see any bullets or knives or food wrappers or dangerous stuff a DCFS worker might write down in her notebook.

Steph followed me into the living room, glanced around, then waited, like I was supposed to take her somewhere else. I walked out of the living room, back through the kitchen, and into the main hallway. First stop was my room. I had never been so glad that I'd stuffed my dirty clothes in the closet.

The pillow and blanket under the bed, though . . .

I bit my nails as Steph asked, "Why are your blinds taped to the windowsill?"

My face flushed. "Um . . . to keep them from blowing when I turn on the fan."

A little-bitty lie. Not enough to send me to hell or foster care. At least, I didn't think so. I might be calling her Steph, but admitting I was a baby and scared of the dark—no.

The house phone rang. I almost ran to my bedside table and snatched it from the cradle. "Hello?"

Nobody answered.

"Hello?"

I heard breathing but no answer. For some stupid reason, I imagined the creep from the store wearing his plaid shirt and munching a hot dog and smiling, holding the phone to his ear and listening to me. It freaked me out. I looked at the caller ID. OUT OF AREA.

Steph took the phone from me and listened. She said,

"Hello?" then checked the caller ID herself and hung up. "Just somebody breathing. Does that happen a lot?"

"No. First time."

A car pulled into the drive, a red Toyota. It was Peavine, Angel, and Ms. Jones. They got out, and Ms. Jones opened the trunk and started handing out cloth grocery bags. She had been to the store. Bless her. And blessing somebody is different from blessing their heart. I would never bless Ms. Jones's heart, because she never did anything dumb except when she rooted for Ole Miss to win college football games against my team, Tennessee, where Dad and Mom went to school.

"Food," I said as brightly as I could, given that I was pretty sure a serial killer had just called my house and breathed through my phone.

Steph smiled when she saw Ms. Jones lugging the groceries toward the door, with Angel just as loaded down and Peavine swinging one bag against each crutch. "Come on," she told me. "Let me see the rest of the place so I can get out of the way and let y'all cook dinner."

CHAPTER 11

Thirteen and One-Half Days After the Fire

Steph and I rushed through Dad and Mom's room and the guest room and my bathroom and theirs, and the guest bathroom. Dad and I kept house pretty well, so stuff seemed clean to me, and nothing looked hazardous, in my opinion. Steph said she liked Mom's taste in decorating and the way Mom used light greens and golds and mirrors to brighten even the dark corners.

I hadn't ever thought about that. Who knew my mom was a good decorator? All I knew was, there was stuff I could touch and stuff I was supposed to leave alone. For the most part, I kept to my bedroom and my parents' room, my bathroom, and the kitchen. Other than that, I went outside, but I didn't say that to Steph. What if she thought *outside* without grown-ups was too dangerous?

When I took her to the basement, she poked her

head in the little bedroom with no windows but didn't turn on the light. After that, she looked at Dad's weights and then the pool table. I winced when I saw brownie wrappers poking out of one of the pool table pockets. A half-eaten peanut-butter sandwich rested on a napkin on the table under the wall rack, and the trash can beside the table was stuffed with juice cartons.

My face went from flush to burn as Steph hunted around the basement, revealing two more of our little trash cans crammed with food wrappers, like Dad and I never took out the garbage. Why had I brought the food down here to eat it in my sleep? My hands went to my stomach. I expected it to be double-size, but it wasn't.

My fingers twitched because I wanted to start cleaning up, but then I might have had to explain why the mess was there, and I couldn't, and I didn't want to say anything about sleepwalking and sleep-eating, because then I might say something about brain tumors and hallucinating and going crazy. I felt dizzy and realized I was breathing shallow and fast, way high in my throat. I relaxed, like the YouTube video had taught me.

Steph didn't mention the mess. She went to the back door instead, unlocked it, opened it, and looked out through the glass storm door. "There's a snake on the pond. Yuck."

"The muddy water draws them," I said, a little squeaky, like an overstuffed mouse. "Snakes love it when you can't see them coming." I walked over and stood beside her long enough to be sure I wasn't lying when I said, "Yep, it's a copperhead. Sorry you took the guns yet?"

"No." She stepped back from the storm door and pushed the main door closed, so we couldn't see the snake. "Do you still have my card?"

"Yes." Whoops. I just added a lie to my list.

"Let me see your phone."

Guilty, I took my phone out of my pocket and handed it to her.

She punched buttons, then handed it back. "There. Now I'm on your contact list. You can call me if you need me, just like Captain Armstrong."

"Thank you," I said, and felt surprised, because I actually meant that.

Upstairs, Peavine and Angel and Ms. Jones started clattering around in the kitchen. I wanted to go upstairs with them, but Steph stopped me by holding up one finger.

"Just a sec. I have one more question, Footer. Please try to be honest, and please try not to get mad, okay?"

I didn't say anything, because every time in my life that a grown-up had told me not to get mad, I hadn't gotten mad. I'd gotten furious. All my muscles tensed before she said a word, and I couldn't stop myself from already feeling a little ticked off.

Steph's expression stayed neutral, and she kept her

voice low as she asked, "Do you think your mother had anything to do with the fire at the Abrams farm?"

Panic flooded me so fast, I almost whimpered. I don't know how I managed to stand still with my heart thundering and my guts twitching, but I did. I even kept looking Steph in the eyes without blinking. I focused on her fake hair and worked hard to remember how much I hadn't liked her when I met her at school. I definitely didn't hate her now, not as much, so that made lying to her more of a problem. But she didn't know anything. She couldn't know anything about the barrette or my hallucinations, because I hadn't told her, and Peavine wouldn't tell my secrets, and nobody else knew, except maybe Angel, and Angel didn't speak to strangers at all, except to quote the Constitution and books about alien mutant rock eaters.

Stay steady. Sound calm. "No. I don't think my mom had anything to do with that fire."

I thought about throwing a fit about how people always assumed Mom did bad stuff because she was mentally ill, but that would have been pushing it.

Because she might have done something.

No.

But . . .

Stop.

I bit the inside of my cheek so I wouldn't start talking to myself out loud in front of Steph, even though I really wanted to.

She studied me without moving while I counted. *One, two, three, four.*

Her brown eyes narrowed.

Five, six, seven, eight, nine.

"Footer, would you tell me if you thought your mother did have something to do with the fire?"

No. "Sure." I didn't even breathe after I told that whopper, and I absolutely wouldn't let myself think about how much bad luck I had piled on my head since Steph walked through the front door today.

"Okay," she said at last, but her sad expression said something completely different.

Bless your heart, Footer Davis. I don't believe you for a minute.

CHAPTER 12

Thirteen and Three-Quarters Days After the Fire

My definition of "best friend": The person who understands that some things just have to be done and does them with you, without arguing, even if you're scared of the dark and might be going crazy, and even if he doesn't know if you're a flower or a rock.

Peavine carried the flashlight, but it didn't do much good.

I gripped the outside of his hand, swinging my arm as his pole moved forward, planted, and then swung again. If I focused on the warmth of his fingers on mine and the cool metal of his crutch touching my wrist, then I wouldn't look at the horrible monster trees grabbing at us from both sides of the path through the woods. I wouldn't think about Angel parked in front of a movie playing on my laptop in my room, something about space aliens and dogs taking over the planet. If she got bored and went to her mom . . .

"We're almost there," Peavine said.

I barely heard him over the frogs and crickets yammering in the darkness. The scent of dew-covered dirt and damp pine made my eyes water. My skin felt clammy even though it was still one thousand degrees two hours after sunset. Ahead of us, the flashlight beam doodled across the absolute darkness as Peavine handled his poles.

We broke tree cover seconds later, but no stars twinkled in the cloudy skies. The flashlight beam scalped the top of ryegrass in the field, eerily still with no breeze to stir it. Peavine led us straight through the tall stalks, down the path we mashed last weekend. We hurried toward the ghostly remains of the Abrams barn, with me stumbling beside him, trying to keep up.

We might have had forever, or we might have had minutes. It depended on when Dad came home, and when Ms. Jones checked on us in my room to be sure we were all sleeping. Peavine and I had gone out the basement door, me to try to figure out once and for all if my mom had been involved in the Abrams mess, and

Peavine because I asked him to go since I was too scared of the dark to head out alone.

If we didn't get back before they realized we were gone, we were so completely dead and grounded. Probably forever.

Peavine slowed, then brought us to a stop. "Here?"

"Yeah." My heart beat so hard, my ribs seemed to rattle. "This is the place."

Everything smelled different in the dark, all wet and moldy. Everything looked different too, just shadows and lumps—but we had come to the right section of the ruins, I was sure of it. This was almost the exact spot where I had hallucinated before. I held my breath, expecting the visions to hit me again right away, but nothing happened.

Pictures, sounds, smells, discussing it—that's what Captain Armstrong told us about how to set off flashbacks. So this should be working already, right?

Why wasn't it working?

I blew out a breath and stubbed my tennis shoe into the ashes.

Maybe I had a brain tumor after all.

"What if you didn't see anything?" Peavine sounded hopeful. "Could be your mind's been playing tricks on you, 'cause you're worried about your mom."

I flinched, because he used the M-word, and he never did that unless I brought it up first. "I saw something. And Stephanie Bridges knows it. She's going to make a stink about Mom unless I figure this out. If I can just remember the truth, then I can tell it, and Mom will get better and come home like always."

"That DCFS lady, she was probably just fishing around, you know?" Peavine moved his crutch and hand away from me and set the flashlight down propped on some dirt, so the beam showed across a swath of burned boards and ashes. "I bet she doesn't really suspect your mom did anything."

"You didn't see her face. You didn't have to lie to her." My words dropped into the darkness, too loud even with the frog and cricket chorus, which sounded distant now that we were out of the woods.

"You weren't lying, Footer." Lightning bugs fired up around Peavine, winking in and out by his shoulders and arms, then farther away, out across the burned ground and the motionless ryegrass. "You really don't know what happened that night, at least not yet, so how could you tell her?"

I didn't want to lie to Peavine, even by accident. It wasn't just the bad luck that lying to my best friend would bring, but how awful I'd feel about it—the kind of awful that would never stop, no matter how much truth I told to make up for it. "It's like snapshots made out of dreams, but I think it's all real. If it isn't real, why is it happening?"

"I don't know." He sounded so patient. He didn't say,

You might be losing it, even though I was thinking that myself. Peavine would never say anything mean to me, even when he should.

"It's like a broken puzzle." I watched the lightning bugs dance and twinkle, pretending to be the night's missing stars. "I have to put it together before somebody accuses Mom of being here during the fire. If Dad thinks she had anything to do with this—well, they'll probably never let her out of the hospital. Mom'll be gone forever."

"Just calm down and think, Footer. You're the smartest girl I know."

That was sweet, especially since his little sister was smarter than both of us. I smiled, then felt sort of glad Peavine couldn't see my face in the dark. "Get hold of my hand again, okay? Don't let go."

"I won't." His palm brushed across my knuckles, and I laced my fingers through his. "So, since the sights and smells aren't doing it and we don't know what sounds to make, try talking about it. That first time this past weekend, what did you see, exactly?"

"Cissy, standing right where you put the flashlight. At first she was just . . . there. Then she had a shotgun, and Mom was with her. They were both holding it." I stared across the yellow beam into blackness broken only by lightning bugs, trying to ignore the part of my brain screaming at me to run.

Just the dark. The dark can't hurt me, I told myself, like

Dad taught me to do. It didn't help much, even when I said it over and over. It seemed like the night was inside my head as much as outside. The harder I tried to look into my own mind, the less I could see.

"My mother talked to Cissy," I told Peavine, so frustrated because we needed to hurry, and I couldn't make the hallucinations come, now that I wanted them. "I think she told her to hurry."

"You let go of me," Peavine said.

"What?"

Peavine's fingertips tapped on my fists, which were raised high. "You're ready to fight, like when you beat on Max Selwin after he knocked me down."

"I—"

Max. The playground. Peavine falling.

A little boy falling . . .

Lightning bugs flickered in the dark, and Peavine flickered away from me.

A tall, thin man stood in front of me with his fists clenched like mine. I could see him because the moon seemed to hang above his mostly bald head, not a full moon, but close to it, and so bright. There were lights, too, on the house and barn, and on poles between the two buildings.

Mom. I was looking for her. I had followed her out of our house, past the pond, and onto the path through the woods. Then she got ahead of me, and I got scared and ran faster. It was so dark and—

My heart stuttered. The man yelled at a boy in front of him. He couldn't see me, because I was standing behind a tree. He couldn't see me, so he yelled and he yelled, and the sound came at me from miles and miles away, like a bad radio broadcast, like the old speakers at school, crackly and fuzzy.

Stupid . . .

Clumsy . . .

Idiot . . .

The boy cried. He was so little. The man shook his fist at the boy.

He can't hit him. If that man hits that boy, the kid might break.

But he did hit him.

Old Mr. Abrams knocked Doc down and stood over the boy, yelling some more.

Mom! *I wanted to call out for her, but the horror, it froze me. This couldn't be real. It wasn't happening. Big men like that didn't bash their fists into tiny little boys and make them scream. I needed to scream. I needed to hit the man. I needed to do* something.

Breathing like a fish thrown out of the water, I shoved myself out from the light pole and charged toward the old man.

He drew back his foot and kicked the boy.

A blast ripped the night in half.

Mr. Abrams didn't fall in slow motion, like people die in the movies. He flew sideways like he'd been hit with a wrecking ball, and he crashed to the ground.

My ears rang. The world winked in and out, in and out, like lightning bugs flashing in a field. Water droplets rained down.

Only it wasn't water.

It wasn't water.

It wasn't. Water.

Pooling on the ground.

Cissy stood in front of me, holding the shotgun. Mom hurried up to her and put her hands over Cissy's on the shotgun, talking to her, maybe trying to get her to let go and give the shotgun to Mom. My ears still rang and buzzed. Nothing made any sense, not the boy on the ground or Mr. Abrams lying there, or Mom or the girl or the shotgun or the not-water covering me.

Hurry . . .

Everything turned to lines and shimmers, and my knees wouldn't hold me.

Fontana? Fontana!

Mom's lips pressed against my forehead. Here, honey. You're in your bed now. *My hair felt wet. My pajamas stuck to me like they did after a bath.* Everything's fine. It was just a dream. You slept through everything. . . .

My eyes closed. My nose stayed full of smoke and fire and blood. I couldn't stop smelling it. I didn't want to smell it anymore. I needed some coffee, like at school. I could smell coffee and stick those molecules in my nose, and the stink of the fire and Mr. Abrams dying might go away.

My eyelids fluttered.

Mom slapped my cheek. Her fingers felt smaller. "Come on, Footer," Peavine said, and the image of Mom standing by my bed shattered into night, and a flashlight beam stabbed my eyes, then went away. Spots floated across Peavine's very worried expression.

"You wake up now," he said. "I'm gonna get Mom or your dad. Footer!"

He flicked the flashlight into my face again, like a doctor trying to examine a patient. "Maybe I should call an ambulance."

"No!" I sat up so fast, I knocked the flashlight out of his hand. I gulped air, and the stench of moldy wet ash made me cough. Then I started crying.

Peavine didn't bother to pick up the flashlight. He just wrapped his arms around me and held me. I pushed my face into his shoulder, into his white T-shirt. He didn't smell like mold. More like soap and puppies.

"What'd you see?" he asked me, squeezing me so tight, I could barely get a breath. "What happened?"

"He blew up. Mr. Abrams blew up."

Peavine pulled back and stared at me, even though the flashlight was pointed at my knee, not my face. "You saw him die?"

"I think so."

"Who shot him?"

"Cissy, I think. Mom was there, and Doc, but Doc

was hurt. Mr. Abrams was beating Doc up."

Peavine hugged me again, this time letting me breathe. "If he was abusing a little boy, somebody should have shot him, then. What a snake."

It's not safe, Fontana. There might be snakes in those ashes. . . .

I cried harder.

Mom burned the snake, my brain whispered. *Mom always burns the snakes we kill.*

"What are you going to do?" Peavine whispered in my ear.

"I don't know," I whispered back.

"You gotta tell your dad. Footer, you gotta do it."

What was I supposed to say? Yes? And let Mom live in some horrible locked, smelly place forever? No? Keep my mouth shut and hide what I knew about arson and murder?

Murder . . .

Oh, God.

Mom.

"I think we better go home," I whispered.

CHAPTER 13

Thirteen and Three-Quarters Days After the Fire, Plus a Few More Minutes

"Dad." I punched his shoulder. "Wake up. I need to talk to you."

Dad made sleepy-troll noises and rolled to his side. I turned on another lamp and tugged the sheet off his head. "Dad, I'm serious."

He still didn't do anything but splutter. I rubbed my sweaty palms on the green sleeping shirt I had slipped into after Peavine and I got back to the house. It wasn't twenty minutes later when Ms. Jones and Angel and Peavine, went home. I didn't think I'd waited that long to try to talk to Dad, but apparently he thought Ms. Jones had already tucked me in, and he was almost all the way asleep already.

"What is it?" Dad's voice sounded like a low groan.

I didn't want to do this. I did *not* want to do this. I rocked onto my toes like I used to do when I was little and scared, then made myself stop. "Peavine and I went back to the Abrams farm tonight."

Dad grunted into his pillow. "I told you to stay away from there. That DCFS worker doesn't care if you and Peavine want to be cops."

"Journalist," I corrected. "Well, me, anyway. But, Dad, we went back because the first time we saw a scary shoe in the woods, and I had a bunch of hallucinations and I probably don't have a brain tumor, since I'm not dead yet, and Angel found a barrette like Mom's."

My hand went to my mouth on reflex, because I hadn't meant to say that much that fast, and the barrette thing . . .

Dad sat up slowly.

I kept my hand on my mouth and watched him, trying not to freak out.

He sighed and stretched, and the sheet fell away from his white T-shirt. It had a stain on the chest, right where a blop of chocolate ice cream might have fallen. When he looked at me, his right cheek was red and his brown eyes seemed bleary and exhausted.

He squinted at me, and I wasn't sure what he was seeing.

"Brain tumor," he mumbled. "And a scary shoe? That would be the scary shoe you e-mailed the Mississippi Bureau of Investigation about? The one you told them might belong to Captain Armstrong?"

My eyebrows lifted. "I sent them a picture."

"They called me at work today."

"Oh." I sat on the edge of the bed next to him.

"They appreciate your efforts to be a good citizen, but they'd rather you not e-mail them anymore without asking me first."

"Okay."

"And, Footer, you realize that if the Mississippi Bureau of Investigation had taken your e-mail seriously, you could have made life very difficult for Captain Armstrong." Dad had his way, way serious face on, and it made me squirm. "He could have been investigated. Embarrassed. Some people in town already aren't too comfortable with him, due to his problems from the war."

Guilt poked directly at my brain, and when I said, "I'm sorry," I really, really meant it.

"It's not me you owe the apology to," Dad said, looking more serious than ever. "Captain Armstrong knows about your e-mail and the photo. He was there, you know. That afternoon. That *was* his shoe in the picture."

I froze in place, totally stunned, and started to ask what Dad was talking about, but he cut me off. "He was trying not to ruin your fun, but he was watching after you because he promised Adele he would, so she'd get in the ambulance. Remember?"

Oh.

Ooooooooh.

Dread and shame settled in my belly like a hot bunch of rocks. I did remember, now that he said it. And I felt kind of awful for forgetting it in the first place.

I was such a—

"Now, that guy you had the school call the police about, the one you called a creep? That wasn't a bad idea. He had a record and he hasn't been out of prison very long—no business being around a school." Dad rubbed his big hand through his hair. "All of that to say, not every wild idea you get is off-base. But, Footer, a little girl lived at the Abrams farm. You know that, right?"

The sheets on Dad's bed felt soft when I picked at them. "Yes, sir."

"Lots of little girls wear barrettes."

Okay, so I had told myself that same thing over and over, and told Peavine, and he had agreed. "But this one looked like a pretzel."

Dad made a sound somewhere between a sigh and a yawn. Maybe it was both. "So do lots of the barrettes you can buy at Walmart. That's where your mother gets hers. I'm sure Cissy Abrams shopped at the same place. It's not like we have a lot of options in Bugtussle."

I couldn't make myself look up from the sheet I was bothering with both hands. "Mom got new barrettes after the fire. She was wearing them when she shot the copperhead."

Dad didn't answer right away. The only sound in the room came from me, my breathing, and my pulling at the sheet's edge.

Finally, Dad said, "Brain tumor." He shook his head, and I could tell he was getting ready to lie down again. "Honey, it's late."

"She might have been there," I whispered, looking away from him and staring at the sheet so hard and totally that my eyes watered. "I think I saw Mom go to the Abrams farm the night of the fire. I think I followed her through the woods."

Dad went quiet again, this time so long that I would have looked at him if I hadn't been scared of seeing his face. When he spoke, his words came out too quiet, like when he was mad and trying not to yell. "You were asleep in your bedroom the whole time. That's what you told me, and what you told the police. It's what your mom told the police too."

"I don't think that's true." I took a deep breath and tried to figure out how to explain the hallucinations. Telling him outright was probably best, even if he thought I needed to go to a hospital, like Mom.

"What's the truth, Footer? Do you even know anymore?"

Dad's questions startled me so badly, I glanced at his face. Both cheeks had turned red, and his mouth made a straight, solid line. He had looked like that when I accidentally caught the backyard on fire, after he'd hugged me and finished hollering about taking dangerous risks and why did I have to try every experiment I ever read about.

Dad's anger punched me right in the heart. In the night, in the dark, with the whole world asleep and Mom gone so far away, I could barely talk to her, I felt like an alien stranded on an ice planet, lost and freezing and completely hopeless.

I shook from the cold inside me. *In my dreams, Cissy shot Mr. Abrams. One of them set the fire that probably killed Cissy and Doc. I think it was Mom.* I looked at Dad and I wanted to say those things, but even as the words played through my mind, they sounded stupid and baby and crazy. I didn't even know what I had seen. They were just hallucinations, nothing real, and nothing with any proof.

"I'm not sure what the truth is," I admitted, "but—"

"Then you better go back to your room," Dad said, still too quiet, talking way too slow. "Get a good night's sleep, and think very, very hard. I want you to consider if what you're telling me is real."

Tears slid from my eyes, and I wiped them away with the backs of my hands. "Okay, but—"

"Footer, this is serious. Do you understand me?"

I had to look away from him, or I would have cried more. "Yes, sir."

"If it's like your walruses and serial killers and brain

tumors and that shoe—knock it off before you really hurt your mother and this family."

"Yes, sir."

I got up from his bed and ran out of his room, back to the hall, and away from his frown and sad eyes. Some part of my mind knew I had left his lights on, but I didn't care very much.

For some reason I didn't even understand, I ran straight to the kitchen and pulled open the pantry. I let the tears wash down my cheeks, and I kept breathing so fast, it made me dizzy, but I couldn't stop as I pulled out a bunch of my lunch drinks and the new jar of peanut butter and the fresh loaf of bread Ms. Jones had brought from the store. I had been eating myself silly in my sleep, right? So maybe it helped me somehow. Maybe it kept the bad dreams away. Maybe it filled up the great big empty I felt with Mom gone, and it was so much bigger now that Dad had sort of left me too.

He didn't believe me. He thinks I'm crazy.

I stared at the sandwich stuff on the counter. This was totally stupid. I knew it, but I couldn't stop myself. If I stopped, I might see Dad's mad face, or Mom lying in her hospital chair babbling about mice and playing the piano she thought she had inside her wrist, or Mr. Abrams blowing into pieces, spraying dark spots all over Cissy and Doc and me and Mom.

Stupid seemed better than any of that.

I went to the fridge and got the jar of grape jelly Mrs. Jones had left us. I got knives and forks and spoons out of the silverware drawer, and paper plates and napkins off the top of the microwave, where Mom kept them. Judging by the messes I made when I sleep-ate, this had to be how I did it—just grab everything and go downstairs and stuff it all down.

Fine. I could do that awake, too. I crammed so much stuff in my arms, I had to use my foot to push down the handle of the basement door and shove it open.

When it banged against the wall, I jumped at the sound. I thought I heard scurrying, scuttling sounds from down in the blackness, but that was just my baby-scared-of-the-dark mind playing goofs on me. I used my shoulder to flip the light switch and chase all the noises away.

I went down one step at a time, like a little kid, so I didn't lose my balance, and I carried all the food to the pool table and spread it out better than a picnic. Then I went back upstairs and got the brownies and cupcakes meant for my lunches, and I took them to the pool table too. I unwrapped enough to fill up three or four plates and then made five peanut-butter-and-jelly sandwiches.

Maybe when I was asleep, I didn't go to this much trouble, but who knew? Might as well make it as fun as possible, since everything else so completely and totally sucked right now. After I got everything arranged, I ate a brownie, stuffing each bite in my mouth and forcing myself to chew it and swallow it, ignoring how much it tasted like sugar-coated cardboard. I choked down one of the sandwiches, but I couldn't face a second one.

Great.

Just great.

Nothing. No help at all. My stomach already hurt. Awake, I couldn't seem to put away as much food as I did in my sleep. I couldn't even make as spectacular a mess. It was kind of disappointing.

And it was time to face the fact that I was losing it, just like Mom.

"Losing it, lost it—not much difference, right?" My voice sounded like a ghost whisper in the silent basement.

I glanced around at the weights, and the shadows they made on the floor. For a time I studied the closed bedroom door and imagined the bed and the little bathroom. I wished I could pretend Mom was in there, just taking a little vacation from the world. Then I could wake her up and ask her if she felt this way when she started going crazy, all confused and empty and sad. Did she think she was letting Dad down, and her friends and me and everybody? Did she try to stop it?

I had wondered those things before, lots of times. I had asked myself if she tried not to get sick, and now I knew. She tried with every bit of strength she had, but it just didn't matter. When sick came, it did what it wanted to do.

That felt like too big a thing to know, so I got under the pool table and curled up, resting my head on the cool wooden pedestal. For the first time ever in my life, I didn't care if the darkness snuck up on me after I fell asleep and covered me like a big blanket full of black, scary nothingness.

I wasn't even sure I wanted to wake up.

CHAPTER 14

Fourteen Days After the Fire

I managed to get back in my own bed before morning. Sometime in the night, I must have eaten the rest of what I had taken down to the pool table, or the dinosaur mice got it, because it was gone. I was surprised I didn't blow up like a beach ball.

School—now, that concept seemed worse than turning into a pool toy, so I told Dad I felt sick. He did the usual stuff, looking in my throat (could he see five peanut-butter-and-jelly sandwiches trying to urp back up?), taking my temperature (can you get a fever from half a box of brownies?), and checking my pulse (maybe juice drinks cause a racing heartbeat?).

"Well," he said after he mashed on the glands in my throat until I gagged, "You don't seem like you're dying, and I don't see any spots or rashes, but you do look pale."

I pulled away from Dad's hands, settled back on my pillow, and shut my eyes, wishing he'd just go away. I didn't want to talk to him, and I didn't want him to sit there looking worried, and I didn't want him to decide he needed to go to the basement before I cleaned up the nasty mess of crumbs and wrappers I had left down there.

"Footer, if I upset you last night, I didn't mean to." Dad sounded worried enough that I almost opened my eyes, but I knew if I did, I'd probably hug him and tell him I didn't mean any of the stuff I said.

I kept my eyes closed.

Dad kissed my forehead. "I love you very much. I just want you to take this stuff about your mom and the fire seriously, okay?"

"Okay," I said back, feeling nothing much but numbness, and like I wanted to burp peanut butter.

"If you have something to tell me now, I'll listen."

Just make sure it's the truth, right? The problem was, I didn't want to lie, and I really, really didn't know what truth I needed to tell. Whatever truth it was, Dad probably didn't want to hear it, no matter what he said.

He waited, like he might be hoping I would say something else. When I didn't, he patted my sheet-covered shoulder. "All right, then. I'll see what I can do about getting somebody to stay with you."

When he got up, I turned over and stared at my white wall.

A few minutes later, Dad came back to my room and said, "Ms. Jones is coming over in five or ten minutes. Will you be okay if I head out so I can stop by the post office on my way to work?"

"I'll be fine," I told the wall.

I felt Dad lay something on the bed beside me. "There's your phone. Call me right away if you need something before she gets here."

I heard my door close. Then I heard the front door close, and the sound of a car engine.

My phone chirped with Peavine's tone. I turned over and picked it up.

R U OK?

Pukey, I texted back, because that was truth enough.

Ew. Feel Betr.

Thks.

Call u latr.

K.

The landline rang. I sat up and got my feet on the floor, dropped my cell on the bed, then shuffled over to my desk. Morning sunlight tried to slice around my blinds, but it barely got in, leaving the room gray and sleepy just like me. The phone rang again, and I picked up the receiver.

"Hello?"

A woman said, "May I speak to Adele Davis, please?" She sounded all official and business-like, probably not one of Mom's support-group people.

I fiddled with the receiver charger. "She's not here. May I take a message?"

"Is Fontana Davis there?"

That made me open my eyes wider. "Um, I'm Fontana."

"Oh, good. You missed your appointment with Dr. Zephram yesterday at three. Do you know if your mother plans to reschedule?"

"Who is this again?"

"Dr. Zephram's office."

"But my doctor is Dr. Ellsworthy."

"Oh, he's a primary care physician. This is a counseling office. Different kind of doctor."

Counseling office? What? I pulled the receiver away and stared at it, then had enough presence of mind to put it back to my ear and say, "Sorry, I don't know anything about Dr. Zephram or what Mom wanted, and I don't know when she'll be back. I'm sure she'll call if she wants to set up another appointment."

"Thank you," the woman was saying as I hung up.

Okay, that was weird. Who were those people? I opened my laptop to look them up online, but my Really Probably Crazy List caught my attention

I stared at it, my fingers hovering above the mouse pad. I knew a lot more now. At least I thought I did. *What's the truth, Footer?* Dad's voice echoed around in my head, pushing tears into my eyes. *What's the truth?*

With a quick click, I closed the document. I didn't know

anything. That's what Dad believed. He was probably right. When I tried to take a breath, it came out all shaky, and I really did feel sick. That's what I got for faking, right?

I thought about closing the laptop, but instead I opened my music and played my favorite song. It didn't make my tears go away. I wanted to call Dad's cell phone and tell him he was a great big huge jerk and he hurt my feelings. Or maybe I just wanted to cry, but if I cried, I'd probably get sick for real.

"I know a lot more now," I said out loud, like Dad could hear me. I imagined him buying stamps as my voice rattled through his ears. I could almost see the way he'd freeze, staring up at the ceiling in shock.

"I do," I whispered.

Then I opened up my Really Probably Crazy List again, and typed fast, banging my fingers on the keys as I changed everything around.

1. Old Mr. Abrams got shot, ~~and nobody knows who shot him.~~ ~~***MOM OR CISSY SHOT HIM WITH A SHOTGUN. WHY?***~~ ***CISSY SHOT OLD MR. ABRAMS WITH A SHOTGUN BECAUSE HE WAS HITTING DOC.***
2. The Abrams farm got burned to the ground, ~~and nobody knows who set the fire.~~ ~~***MOM OR CISSY SET THE FIRE. WHY?***~~ ***MOM PROBABLY SET THE FIRE, MAYBE TO COVER UP WHAT CISSY DID.***

3. Cissy and Doc might be dead or alive, and nobody knows where they are. ***BUT THEY MIGHT HAVE DIED IN THE FIRE BY ACCIDENT.***
4. Mom ~~might have been~~ ***WAS MOST DEFINITELY*** there.
5. I ~~might have been~~ ***WAS MOST DEFINITELY*** there.
6. ~~Somebody might have been watching us while we searched.~~ ~~***THE SOMEBODY HAD SHOES LIKE CAPTAIN ARMSTRONG.***~~ ***CAPTAIN ARMSTRONG WAS WATCHING US BECAUSE HE TOLD MOM HE WOULD.***
7. ~~I might be~~ ~~***PROBABLY AM***~~ ~~crazy.~~ ***I MIGHT BE CRAZY, BUT I SAW ALMOST EVERYTHING.***

It was hard to look at the items now, because I was pretty sure I was right about all of them, and I was pretty sure Dad would never believe me. I hit save before I could chicken out and delete everything. I'd come back later and clean it up and explain stuff better. Then I'd send a copy to Peavine. He'd believe me. Peavine would never call me a liar or treat me like I was crazy. After everything went so wrong with Dad and Mom, too, that felt really, really important.

Somebody knocked on the front door.

Perfect.

Was this my punishment for staying home when I didn't have the runs or a bad one-hundred-and-three fever? I rubbed one eye, then the other. I really didn't feel like talking to missionaries or answering a survey. It might be the postman or the UPS woman or the FedEx guy. Whatever it was, they could leave it on the porch.

I decided not to answer the knock and stared at my list some more. Then I started feeling cold, and I couldn't help looking over my shoulder, out into the hall.

What if somebody important had been at the door?

What if a serial killer had been at the door?

Okay, that was stupid.

But . . .

I got up and went to the front door, stood on my tiptoes, and peeked outside. Nobody was there. After a few seconds I turned all the locks and put on the chain. Then I stared at the closed door for a long time, worrying. Blood rushed in my ears, making it hard to think. Was the basement door locked? I couldn't remember.

Stop scaring yourself.

But I couldn't help it. Where was my phone? I ran my hands up and down my sleeping shirt even though I knew it didn't have pockets. On my bed. I left it in my room.

This was completely idiotic. I had nothing to be scared of. Stuff like this—it was why Dad didn't trust me. Because I could act like such a baby.

Something thumped in the basement.

I let out a squeak and ran to my room and grabbed my phone off the bed, barely breathing as I unlocked its screen. The house had gone tomb quiet.

My fingers pushed 9-1-1, but I hesitated before I pressed send. If I called the dispatch center, they'd send a bunch of people, and Dad would know, and he'd be so pissed with me. He might even get in trouble for leaving me alone while Peavine's mom drove over here.

I inched over to my window, pried loose one blind, and peeked out. Still nobody out there. I held my breath and counted to five, and I didn't hear any noises, either.

My gaze shifted back to the numbers I had dialed, and I heard Dad's voice in my head, sounding sad and angry. *What's the truth, Footer? Do you even know anymore?*

I bit my bottom lip. Then I deleted the 9-1-1 and picked Captain Armstrong from my contact list instead.

He sounded asleep when he answered, but when I told him I was home sick and waiting for Ms. Jones and somebody knocked on the front door and scared me, I saw him come straight out his front door wearing a bathrobe, phone to his ear. He held his free hand above his eyes to shield them from the sun, and he stared down our road.

He studied the scene, and then he said, "It was church people, Footer. I see them on down the road, putting pamphlets in people's mailboxes. Now they're knocking on somebody else's door."

"Okay." I relaxed a fraction. "Thanks."

"I'll keep a watch until Ms. Jones gets here. You don't have to worry."

"Thanks, Captain Armstrong." I started to tell him good-bye, then hesitated, feeling the bloom of all that hot guilt in my stomach. Here he was being nice to me, and I hadn't been good to him at all, treating him like a real suspect and giving his name to the MBI, and acting like some people in town did, like he was all dangerous and mean, when he wasn't.

My fingers gripped the phone, then relaxed, gripped and relaxed. I tried to get my breath and find the right words.

"You okay there, kid?" Captain Armstrong asked.

"I—yes. Thank you. I'm just . . . it's . . . I'm sorry I asked you stuff about the war and took a picture of your shoe. I know the rumors around town aren't true, about you and the fire. I always knew that."

There was a long pause, and the heat in my stomach got ten times worse. I felt it moving up into my chest, my throat, my face.

"I don't know what else to say," I whispered. "I don't know what to do, except be sorry, even if it's not enough."

"It's enough," he said, and he didn't sound cold or angry like I thought he would. "Sometimes when you really slip up in this world, sorry's all you've got. It has to be enough. I'm not mad at you, Footer. I never was."

"Okay," I said. I thanked him again and hung up, but I stood there awhile, watching the captain through my window, hoping he really meant what he said about not being mad at me.

He had believed me about somebody knocking on the door, at least. He had believed what I told him, even though my own father didn't.

Why did that make me sad instead of happy?

CHAPTER 15

Still Fourteen Days After the Fire

Once I was pretty sure no serial killer was trying to break into my house, I changed into shorts and a shirt, crammed my phone in my pocket, and sat on my bed. My heart wasn't beating fast anymore, and my breathing sounded like a person now instead of a half-strangled chicken, and I wasn't feeling as guilty about sort of being mean to Captain Armstrong.

As for Dad . . .

My chin dropped toward my chest and I sat there staring at nothing, feeling really sad and completely alone. It was like being in the dark with all the lights on. "Alone" dug at me just like "scared" did, when the lights were off and I couldn't see anything at all.

I wasn't a baby. I wasn't.

But I wanted my mother.

Great, big empty "alone" swelled around me like some awful balloon, taking all the air. I wanted to see Mom, but not sick, staring, crazy Mom. I wanted smiling Mom, happy Mom, with-me Mom. Crying was stupid, but I did it anyway, letting the tears roll down my face and not even wiping them off. Wiping tears was what moms did, and right now I didn't have mine.

My eyes moved to my bedroom door and into the hall, and I looked at my parents' bedroom door. I wasn't supposed to go in there without them, or unless they asked me to, or unless I asked. Privacy and respect and all that stuff.

But it was Mom's room. If I opened the door and went inside, I might smell her or grab some bit of her and be able to hold on to it until she got better and came home.

I wiped my face with both hands, and I went down the hall and through the closed door. For a few heartbeats I just stood there, breathing in and out, in and out, but all I could smell was the light pine scent of dad's aftershave, with hints of soap from his shower that morning, and the minty tang of toothpaste. The tears came back again.

Mom had a desk near the window, just like me, only she kept the blinds up, not down. Even though it felt really wrong and really weird, I wanted to look through her things. I wanted to touch them.

Sunlight streamed through the windowpanes, showing all the dust on stacks of recipe books, boxes of stationery, notebooks, appliance manuals, and clipped-together bills. The stacks felt like proof that Mom wasn't always sick. They seemed to say, *See? Look. She organized me. She knew what she was doing.*

I walked over to the desk, put my hand on the nearest stack, and took a deep breath. My heart thumped when the air swept into my nose, because it smelled a little like her rosy perfume.

Mom. There you are.

My chest hurt.

I could see her sitting there at the desk, smiling to herself as she wrote down instructions for some disgusting fancy dinner dish, or scrawled a letter to somebody, because yes, my mom still sent snail mail.

The top box of stationery was powder-blue paper with lines on it. I opened the box and ran my fingertips across the silky surface. So soft, and it smelled even more like her. Mom had pretty handwriting. I could almost imagine the loopy letters she'd make as she wrote *Fennel Meatloaf* or *Arugula Muffins* or *Carrot Ice Cream.*

Blech.

I smiled.

Then I frowned.

It didn't make sense, how Mom could be so completely fine sometimes, sitting here in this room, working at this desk—or so sweet and nice that she fed yard squirrels and basement mice her breakfast—and then end up a drooling zombie in the hospital, miles and miles away from us.

My hands wandered across the desktop, sliding pieces of Mom's life and mind and heart back and forth. Fresh tears made me see everything in prisms and rainbows. I wanted to be mad at her for leaving us, mad like I always used to be, when I was really little. Mad would feel better than . . . than whatever made my chest weigh ten-thousand pounds and hurt so much.

Maybe I don't have a brain tumor. Maybe I have a heart tumor. If I had a heart tumor, I'd so be dead by morning. But then I wouldn't be here when Mom got home. I didn't really want to have any kind of tumor at all.

I opened the center drawer of Mom's desk. Nothing there but pens and pencils and paper clips and thumbtacks and rubber bands. I opened the only left-hand drawer and found more boxes of stationery, all different colors, some thumb drives with rubber protectors shaped like pigs and dogs, a flashlight, some matches, and emergency storm candles. The top drawer on the right had a weather radio, which figured, because when Mom wasn't obsessing about snakes, she worried about tornados, like everyone else in Mississippi.

It took me a while to realize I was smiling and the tears weren't falling anymore.

In the drawer underneath that, I found a bag of lemon drops, two unopened bottles of Mom's medication, and three letters addressed to Mom from Carl Abrams at

Central Mississippi Correctional Facility down in Pearl.

Oh. My. God.

My breath caught, and I swiped the remnants of tears out of my eyes with the backs of my hands. When I picked up the letters and examined them, I realized they had been opened, then tucked back in their envelopes and fastened together with one of Mom's yellow paper clips. I took off the paper clip.

"Carl Abrams," I said out loud, looking at the paper like I could X-ray-vision the person who'd sent them. I had seen his face before, because the papers and television news had shown him over and over, after the fire. The news people all said Cissy and Doc's dad was still locked up and would be for at least two more years.

I pulled open the first letter, which was dated December of last year. It was short, and written in blocky print.

Dear Ms. Davis,

I dont read so good, so people got to help me undistand what you said, and help me spell my words on this note. Thank you for doin the naborly thing when my mom died and taking my dad and kids some food. I'm real glad you realized somthin not right there, and went back more and more to see my babies. It hurts my heart to know what they go thru. I thought my dad would have got better when he laid off the drinking, but I guess not. I let them down so bad, bein stupid and using that awful stuff and getting myself locked in this hole. I got two years left on my time, but I go to my meetings and I been clean for fourteen months. Tell my kids I come to get them just as soon as I am out of here with a job and can feed them.

Yours in Jesus,

Carl Abrams

I folded the letter and put it back in its envelope. The second letter was dated February 10, from this year.

Dear Ms. Davis,

I met with the parole board but they dont give me no time off even though my kids need me. They didn't take none of that serious. They say if my kids is having trouble I should call the law on my dad. You say you tried that when you was little. So did I. We both know how that don't work out good.

You tell that old SOB he touch my kids again, Il come for him and he be real sorry then.

Yours in Jesus (I think Jesus be okay with me smackin him down if its to help kids),

Carl Abrams

The landline rang.

I jumped, then ignored the receiver on Mom's desk until it stopped. I didn't even look at the caller ID. I just put the second letter away and went to the third, opening it despite the way my hands trembled. It was dated two weeks before the fire.

Mom, what did you do? What's all this about?

Dear Ms. Davis,

Sorry my old man talked rough to you. Thats how he is and always was. With what you say about your own folks, guess you understand that, and how a man gets to be like me. Glad you was able to be stronger than I was.

I cant thank you enough for them pictures of my girl and boy. I send you one back of me here that a cowboy took for me with his phone cause he is new and dont know no better and he is still nice. Most guards get mean after a while workin in this place. Cant say I blame em.

Tell Cissy girl she is brave and tell little man Doc that his dad loves him and will come as soon as he can.

Yours in Jesus,

Carl Abrams

My brain turned in circles as I put the third letter back in its envelope, then shut it in Mom's drawer. Like images from an old projector, pictures flickered through my awareness as my ears started to buzz, and my nose filled with the stench of smoke.

The old man, Mr. Abrams, with his fist doubled up, ready to punch the little boy, Doc . . .

The few times Mom had talked about her own family,

and how she had to get away, because they were mean and no-good and God hadn't seen fit to make medicine for mean and no-good yet . . .

Mr. Abrams hitting that tiny little kid . . .

Cissy and Mom with the shotgun . . .

It seemed so wrong, that Carl Abrams knew how much his kids needed him, that he wanted to help them so much, but he couldn't. He was trapped by whatever he had done in the past, locked up a long way from them, just like Mom had been locked away from me and Dad. The tears came back, and they slid down my cheeks, and my heart tumor got twice as big.

Why did stuff like this have to happen?

I knew I should put the letters down, but I couldn't. I got tears on them, and they weren't even mine.

The phone rang again, and finally, finally, I managed to let go of the letters. My hand moved toward the receiver, slow-motion, not real, not even seeming like it was part of my body. I didn't feel like I was on the planet. I didn't feel like a person.

Robot me picked up the phone, still staring at the drawer where I'd put the tear-stained letters. My eyes drifted to the caller ID, which said OUT OF AREA.

"Hello?"

"Can I talk to Adele Davis, please?"

A woman, like the one who called a few nights ago. Maybe even the same one—but this time she sounded weird, slurring her words so bad, I barely understood them.

"Who is this?" I asked in my flat robot voice. "Who are you?"

"You must be her girl. Farah or some such, right?"

That last word came out as *riiiite*—her accent was worse than Peavine at his maddest. "I'm Footer," I muttered. "And you are?"

The woman sucked in a breath, then blew it out slow, like some old movie star smoking a cigarette. "Look, you tell your mama I can't do it. Got that?"

"Can't do what?"

"I won't be calling again, and she don't need to call me, either. I'm changing my number."

"Can't do what?" I repeated, but the slurring, smoking woman hung up.

Like an idiot, I stood there, hoping she'd pick back up, but the line clicked and the dial tone started.

I put the receiver back on the charger, still not feeling connected to my own self or my fingers or the desk or the world. I stood there so long, I was still in the same spot when Ms. Jones got there. She found me, took one look at me, and shooed me back to my own room.

Walking wasn't as hard as I thought it was going to be. I went without arguing or tripping or falling, but I took a notebook and pen from my desk before I climbed into bed.

Ms. Jones fussed with the covers, talking about making

me a breakfast that would probably make me throw up a week's worth of brownies and peanut-butter-and-jelly sandwiches. Then she said, "You really miss your mom, don't you?"

I blinked at Ms. Jones, who looked way too much like Peavine for me ever to say something crosswise to her. *Which Mom?* I wanted to ask. *The nice one who cooks disgusting lemon-pepper asparagus and smiles while she works at her desk, or the secret Mom who listens to secret things from other kids, writes to men in prison, makes counseling appointments for me that she doesn't tell anybody about, and maybe sets fires that burn people to death?*

Out loud, I said, "Yes, I miss Mom. I'll probably be sick until I get to visit her again."

"I see." Ms. Jones stroked my cheek once and nodded, her brown eyes full of that total understanding only she and Peavine could radiate. "I'll be sure to tell your father. Maybe he can work something out."

From the Notebook of Detective Peavine Jones

Interview of Peavine Jones, by Angel Jones, Fourteen Days After the Fire

Location: My Butthead Brother's Nastified Bedroom

> Butthead: This is stupid. I don't know anything about the fire. I'm investigating it, remember?
>
> Me: You and Footer said all suspects should be interviewed and that everyone is a suspect. That means you have to do this.
>
> Butthead: Then I should interview you.
>
> Me: Duh. We were with Mom at church.
>
> Butthead: Fine. Whatever. Just get this over with.
>
> Me: Do you like Footer, or do you like her?
>
> Butthead: What does that have to do with the fire?
>
> Me: Nothing. I just want to know.
>
> Butthead: I'm only doing this so you don't go screaming to Mom that I'm being mean to you. Everything's not simple black and white like you think.
>
> Me: I'm not simple black and white.
>
> Butthead: Of course you're not. You read books fatter than my head.

Me: So, do you like Footer?
Butthead: [Suspect seems anxious. See? I sound more like a detective than he does.] I do like Footer. I missed her when she didn't come to school today. I'm worried about her now, but I can't go to her house Saturday, because her dad's taking her to Memphis to see her mother.
Me: How was she when you called her tonight?
Butthead: She didn't sound right. She acted kinda far away, and she couldn't get her words to come out in a straight line. I think she misses her Mom more than ever, but she hates it when I try to ask her about stuff like that. I think what she remembered about the fire at the Abrams farm is stressing her out way too much.
Me: Tell Mom.
Butthead: I can't. Footer would get mad.
Me: Tell her dad, then. So what if she gets mad?
Butthead: I should have talked to Mr. Davis myself. He didn't believe Footer about what she remembered, but he didn't see her remember it. I did. Plus, he hasn't seen the list Footer made when she stayed home. She

e-mailed it to me about an hour ago.

Me: What list?

Butthead: Never mind. I shouldn't have said anything.

Me: Oh, this list. The one on your printer.

Butthead: Give me that, you little snot!

Me: You wish.

Mystery Puzzle, Worked Out by Footer Davis

By Footer Davis

1. Mom started going over to the Abrams farm when Ms. Abrams died, and kept going because she realized something bad was happening there. Cissy and Doc Abrams must have told Mom they were being abused by their grandfather. That's why she wouldn't take me with her. I know she would have tried to help them, because Mom went through bad stuff when she was little too.

2. Mom wrote Carl Abrams at the prison down in Pearl and told him Cissy and Doc needed him.

3. Carl Abrams answered her. I read the letters. They're in Mom's desk drawer. He said he couldn't come save his kids until he got out of prison and got a job. He sounded like a nicer guy than I thought he'd be.

4. I know I was at the farm the night the fire happened, because the smoke molecules stayed in my nose, like that coffee experiment we did in class. Mom gave me a bath and put me to bed. She told me I slept through everything, but the stench was too strong to be floating on the wind from half a mile away, and

besides, I never open my windows. You know that, and you know why.

5. The night of the fire, old Mr. Abrams hit Doc and knocked him down, and then he kicked him. Cissy shot Mr. Abrams to keep him from killing Doc.

6. Mr. Abrams blew apart right in front of me. I want to quit seeing it in my head. Captain Armstrong was right about not wanting to think about bad stuff like that.

7. Mom tried to make me a counseling appointment. I missed it because I didn't know about it. She probably did that because I saw somebody get exploded by a shotgun blast, and she thought it would make me sick like her. Maybe it has.

8. Mom probably set the fire to hide what Cissy did. Then something went wrong, and Cissy and Doc accidentally died in the fire. I didn't see that part.

9. Some woman called to tell Mom she couldn't do something. She sounded drunk or high. I think it might have been somebody Mom called about Cissy and Doc. I think it might have been their mother, but I have no idea.

10. The barrette Angel found must have been Mom's. I know it, and I think Dad knows it too, but he doesn't want to think about it, because it's proof she was there. I'm not talking to him about it anymore, not after last night. I thought about telling your mom or Ms. Malone or Captain Armstrong or even Stephanie Bridges, but I don't think they'd believe me. I don't even know if I want them to believe me.

11. I'm going to go talk to Mom. She has to tell me the rest of what happened. It's time to know.

CHAPTER 16

Fifteen Days After the Fire

Mom could focus her thoughts enough to walk on her own, so she didn't need the rolling recliner chair anymore. Her hair had been combed and pulled back into a ponytail, and somebody had helped her put on a little makeup. She had on her own clothes too—jeans and an orange Tennessee Volunteer Nation jersey with sleeves that stopped at the elbows, and orange sneakers. She would have looked pretty normal as she came to the visiting room off her unit, if it hadn't been for the nurse walking her, holding her arm to help with balance.

I watched Mom's feet drag as much as move, and I felt sick inside. I had gotten used to what she looked like as she got ill, right before she got sent to the hospital, and what she looked like when she came home. I had even gotten a little used to watching her slide toward nutty thinking and not be able to take care of herself when she quit taking her pills. This in-between-sick-and-getting-well phase—I hadn't seen it before, and it made me sad.

Dad hugged Mom when she got to the doorway of the room, and she hugged him back. He kissed the top of her head with his eyes closed and thanked the nurse for looking after her. Then the nurse walked her in to me and eased her down on one of the small two-seat couches. The air went out of the plastic cushion, and it sounded so much like a fart, I had to smile.

Mom smiled too, but her mouth didn't go all the way up at the corners. Her eyes settled on me, but they didn't focus. When she quit smiling, her lips sagged, and I worried that she might drool. She put both hands on the couch, like she had to hold herself up to keep from falling.

"She's had her morning meds," the nurse told me. "She may be a little drowsy, but that'll pass." Then she slipped out of the visiting room to go talk to Dad, and she closed the door behind her.

"I hate the way these pills make me feel," Mom said.

The room was too cold, like rooms in hospitals always were. I rubbed my hands together to keep feeling in my fingers as I said, "I know. But you don't do so good without them. Last time I was here, you thought you had a piano in your wrist."

Mom lifted her arm and gazed down at it. "Huh. That's a new one."

She didn't remember. She usually didn't remember the really crazy stuff later, when she started getting well.

"Sharks and barracudas," she muttered, but that wasn't nutty stuff. She was talking about a picture she showed me once, the emblem of one of her support groups. The picture showed a person on a tightrope trying to get across a pool labeled LIFE. On one side, a big shark named ILLNESS swam, mouth open. On the other side, hoards of barracudas labeled SIDE EFFECTS waited to eat the person if she tripped.

The group talked a lot about needing options better than the shark or the barracudas and pushing scientists to find cures instead of more treatments to make drug companies rich. I didn't understand all that, but I knew it had something to do with why I found Mom's medication in places like her desk drawer because she hadn't taken it.

Mom lifted her arm so I could see her wrist. Her arm and hand shook rhythmically, back and forth. "No piano," she said, and tried to smile again.

"So that probably was just your sickness talking?" I asked, because I hadn't been able to figure out anything the piano might have meant or stood for.

"Probably just the crazy," Mom agreed.

"Don't call yourself crazy," I told her.

She nodded but didn't say anything, and looked totally exhausted.

The sick sensation inside me threatened to turn into

actual nausea. How could I ask Mom the questions I needed to ask? She wasn't even all the way Mom again. What if I made her sicker and she had to stay longer? What if she got upset and just fell over and busted her head or something?

I went over to one of the chairs and pulled it around until I was facing Mom. When I sat, our knees almost touched. There. At least I could catch her if I had to. Why didn't that make me feel any better?

Mom's shaky hand patted my leg. "So, how's it going, honey?"

"I miss you," I whispered, then got mad at myself, because I wanted to cry.

"I miss you, too." A tear dribbled out of Mom's eye, and I *really* wanted to cry then, but I couldn't. Me starting to sob would bring Dad and the nurse running. I made fists and dug my fingertips into my palms.

The almost-pain kept me steady enough to say, "We're having some trouble, Dad and me. He didn't speak to me the whole way here. We listened to the radio instead."

Mom's eyebrows pulled together, and her saggy smile turned into a frown. "That's not like him."

Deep breath. In, out. In, out. I could do this. I had to do this. "Dad's mad because I tried to tell him about what I remembered from the night of the fire."

Mom twitched like I'd hit her with lightning. "We don't need to talk about that, honey."

Her eyes glazed, and she went away. "Did you feed the mice, baby?"

"Yeah, sure." I knew better than to argue with her about stuff I didn't have to. Even with me humoring her, it took a full ten seconds for her to come back into the room with me.

Once I could tell she was back again, I tried a different direction. "Why did you make me a counseling appointment with Dr. Zephram's office?"

"I—I'm not sure." She didn't twitch this time, but she was lying. She wouldn't meet my eyes, and her face screwed up like she had gas.

I could see part of the fading green bruise on her shoulder, from when she shot the snake. Maybe if I didn't watch her face when I hurt her, I could keep going. "Did you think I might have problems because of what I saw? You were right. It was bad, and really gross."

Another twitch.

"I'm sorry, Footer," she whispered, then lost focus.

I shrugged, trying to play it as no big deal.

When Mom touched my leg again, I let my eyes trace her fingers, trying to ignore the tremors from her medication. "I know Cissy shot Mr. Abrams, and I know why. Did you set the fire?"

Mom's fingers gripped my knee hard enough to make me wince. "Doesn't matter," she muttered. "The snake is dead. Let him stay dead, okay?"

The room's cold seeped into my skin, my muscles, my bones, until I froze solid, sitting there in front of Mom. I even imagined her hand frosted to my leg. When I met her gaze, we turned into ice statues together, except for her shaking.

Don't ask me anything else, her green eyes pleaded.

"A woman called," I told her, my lips numb. "She sounded pretty out of it, and she said to tell you she couldn't do it. Was that Cissy and Doc's mother?"

Slowly, slowly, Mom nodded.

"I read the letters from their dad, the ones in your desk drawer. I'm sorry I went into your room. I just missed you so bad. I didn't even mean to be snooping, but now I really have to know—I *need* to know—if I'm starting to get sick. If none of this stuff in my head that I'm remembering actually happened, if I'm making it all up, then I need to see a doctor and get medicine."

This made Mom look confused, and not in a sick way—more normal, everyday perplexed. "You're not getting sick."

My muscles went suddenly loose, and I realized just how tight they had been the second before. And then Mom was looking at me again, really looking at me, and we both knew I had to ask. I saw it in the way her expression started to melt to sadness and fear, and the way her mind seemed to be trying to run away from me again, before I could get out the words.

"Did Doc and Cissy die in the fire, Mom?"

Mom's mouth quivered. Then her whole body shook.

I wanted to smack my head with my hands. I sort of wanted to smack her, too, but I felt awful about that. "Please. You have to tell me the rest of what happened."

"No!" she yelled, and let go of me and pounded her hands on the couch, her eyes flipping from unfocused to terrified so fast that I didn't see it coming. I shoved my chair backward, even though I knew she wouldn't hurt me. I hadn't ever seen her so upset, and it was my fault. I did it. I knew something like this would happen—but I did it anyway.

I had to. No, I didn't. "Mom!"

Dad and the nurse burst into the visiting room.

Mom sobbed, hitting the couch over and over again. "Leave it alone, leave it alone, leave it alone!"

Tears washed down my face as I got out of my chair, and I started apologizing and telling her over and over that I would leave everything alone, because I didn't know what else to do.

"Sorry," Dad said to the nurse, or maybe to Mom or to me—I couldn't tell. "Adele, take it easy." He picked me up like I was five, holding me to him as he backed out of the room, keeping me faced away from Mom.

The nurse spoke to her in low tones as we moved into the hall. "That's it. Let it out. Let it all out of you. Just hit the couch."

Dad turned to walk down the hospital corridor, and I could see Mom over his shoulder. She stared at me and stopped hitting the furniture, and her face focused again, and she cried harder. Then she leaned forward, put her face in her hands, and started rocking.

My stomach tied itself into a hundred knots. I squirmed in Dad's grip as he hurried away. "Wait. Let me talk to her. I shouldn't have asked her anything. It's my fault. Let me go! Please, Dad, it's all my fault. We can't leave her like this. It's my fault!"

Dad kept walking, holding tighter to me. "Your mom isn't anybody's fault," he said into my ear. "She's just not ready yet."

She'll never be ready, will she? Because she probably set that fire and accidentally killed those kids. This time, she's never coming home.

And it was my fault. Dad didn't understand. I balled up my fists and hit his shoulders like Mom had hit the couch. He didn't stop walking.

Mom receded, getting smaller and smaller, until the visiting-room door closed and Dad turned a corner and I couldn't see my mother anymore.

From the Notebook of Astronaut Angel Jones

Because When I Am an Astronaut, Journalists Will Need Notes for My Biography

My Notebook Will Be a Lot Better Than My Brother's Notebook.

I Don't Remember When the Fire Was Exactly. Sorry.

> All Me: My brother's sweet on Footer Davis.
> They'll probably get married when they're old and ugly.
> I grabbed Footer's list off my brother's printer.
> I gave the list and the barrette to Mom.
> Mom is taking the list and the barrette to Mr. Davis.
> The police need to talk to Ms. Davis again.
> Everybody needs to stop pretending.
> Pretending should only be in books with dragons and knights and wizards.
> If I was a wizard, I'd make it so people never got hit or murdered or burned.
> I am not going to be a wizard. I am going to be an astronaut.

CHAPTER 17

Fifteen Long, Endless Days After the Fire

Dad: I don't even know what to say to you about this list.

Me: Am I in trouble?

Dad: I think we're all in trouble now.

I thought it had been awful making Mom so upset like that, then having to leave her.

It was five hundred times more awful seeing Dad upset.

He didn't believe me. Not about any of it. He thought I was exaggerating. And the sad painted all over his face—he thought I was imagining things like Mom does, and that I just didn't understand what kind of disaster I was creating.

After Ms. Jones came over and gave him my list and

the barrette, then left, Dad called the station where he worked. I sat on the kitchen floor hugging my knees and thinking about how I never wanted to talk to Peavine or Angel ever again, how Dad didn't want to talk to me anymore, and how Mom didn't want to talk to anybody.

How could Peavine have let Angel get her hands on that list? He knew how she was. He knew she wouldn't keep it private. Why didn't he get it back from her? He was my friend. My *best* friend. I should have been able to tell him anything and trust that he'd keep it safe from Angel.

The thought of not talking to him made my insides hurt from loneliness.

Peavine let Angel snatch my list, and when she gave it to their mom, he didn't try to talk her out of worrying about it. He told our secrets. And now those secrets were right here, surrounding Dad and me like shadows with fangs, waiting to bite us to death.

Dad hung up the phone. He didn't look at me when he wiped his cheeks with a hanky, or when he tucked the hanky back in his jeans pocket. For a few moments he stood staring at the sink, both hands on his orange T-shirt, the one from Tennessee's national championship year.

I would have given anything for it to be fall, with a football game coming on. We could watch it together and yell at referees and eat popcorn, and maybe, somehow, all of this would go away, or at least get better.

Would he ever watch football with me again?

"They'll be here in a while," Dad said. "I'm going out to mow."

"But it's almost dark," I whispered.

Dad walked out of the kitchen like he hadn't heard me. I knew "they" meant other police officers from where he worked. As for the mowing, it was Saturday in Mississippi, and it was summertime. Everybody had to mow if they didn't want to live in a jungle. He might could get a little done before it got pitch black. Besides, Dad liked to mow when he needed to relax or work something out in his head—like where he was going to lock his wife up forever after she got charged with murdering two kids, so she couldn't hurt anybody else, or maybe where he'd send his daughter, too, since she wasn't much better off, bless her heart.

I didn't have any tears left, so I didn't cry. Instead I thought about my mother rocking and rocking and rocking. I rocked too, back and forth, to see if it made me feel any better.

It didn't.

I kept laying out the mystery pieces in my mind and rearranging them to see if they'd turn out differently.

They didn't.

My eyes moved to the pantry. I could try stuffing myself silly, but I didn't think that would help either. All those shelves full of food, sitting just in front of me, behind the closed door. No light got in there. It would be dark. Whatever lived in the dark and wanted to eat me, it could be in that pantry.

But that was stupid. I didn't even get a little bit scared. If I opened that door, I'd just find the food. There wouldn't be anything right in front of me that I couldn't see.

Right?

My hands moved to my belly, which hadn't gotten as big as a beach ball.

I looked at my hands and thought about my memories from the fire, how they hadn't been there, and then they were. They had been inside my mind the whole time, but I hadn't let myself see them. I wasn't any better than Dad, refusing to see what I couldn't handle.

Great.

Mom's craziness and Dad's stubbornness. I really got the best of both parents in my genetic structure, didn't I?

What else was I refusing to see?

Something clattered in the basement.

Fear hit me like a cold wave, and my whole body froze solid. I listened to the sound of my breathing, and it sounded so, so loud in the quiet house.

Way out in the distance, a thousand miles away, the riding mower started, nothing but a distant growl. Shadows grew in the room as the day went away, and my heart went stutter-stutter-stutter and I took my really loud breaths and I listened. I listened so hard, my ears ached.

Nothing but the mower.

I looked from my stomach to the pantry to the basement door.

Was there something down there?

Right. Dinosaur mice. Of course there was nothing in the basement. I really did make stuff up. I was getting just like Mom, worrying about things that didn't even exist.

The Abrams kids existed. They had real problems, and she tried to help. I thought about the creep at the school. Like Mom, I wasn't wrong *all* the time. No. In fact, I was right a lot of the time. Maybe I didn't have brain tumors or chest tumors or stalking walruses, but that guy at the school—he really had been a bad guy.

Downstairs in the basement, something went *thump*.

I shut my eyes.

"Not real," I told myself out loud, like that would help. "Not real, not real, not real."

Thump.

I breathed faster and faster. Mice? Dead squirrel ghosts? Serial killers? Walking tumors? Homicidal walruses? I smacked myself in the side of the head, and the sting made me open my eyes wide. And a little wider.

I thought about Dad, outside mowing. He wasn't far. I could go get him, but he'd totally think I was being crazy. Calling 9-1-1 was out of the question unless a walrus exploded out the basement door and tried to stick its white straw tusks through my heart. If I called Captain Armstrong, Dad would have a fit.

Peavine . . .

No.

I swallowed down a lump in my throat, feeling more alone than I had ever felt in my whole entire life.

After a few more seconds I slid my phone out of my pocket, found Stephanie Bridges on my contact list, and called her.

"Hey," I muttered when she answered.

"Footer?" She sounded shocked, but also happy, like she actually wanted to hear from me. "What's going on?"

"I—" *What? I'm sure there's a monster in my basement? I can't handle being this scared? I'm a total baby?*

From way down in the basement came a very definite *thump*. Dad's mower sounded farther away than ever. I felt like a concrete statue, set right into the floor.

"Talk to me, Footer," Steph said.

"I miss my mom," I said. And I started to cry.

Steph took a breath, very slowly, in and then out, while I stared at the basement door and waited for it to open.

"I know you do." Steph sounded sympathetic and not fake.

"I'm scared she'll never come home," I told Steph, staring at that door. "I'm scared my dad thinks I'm crazy. I'm scared he'll never listen to me about anything ever again, but there really is something in the basement."

This time she breathed fast and sharp, like me. "Where is he?"

"Way in the back, out mowing."

"Go get him."

"No."

"Footer—"

"No!"

I babbled out why—about the list I sent Peavine and how he let Angel steal it, and how the police were coming soon, and how Mom would probably go to prison forever for accidentally killing Cissy and Doc Abrams, and how Dad looked at me before he went outside, and how I was hearing the noises.

I worried Steph would blow me off like Dad did, but she said, "You're kidding." Then, "No, you're not kidding, because nobody could make all that up." And then, "Go to your room and lock your door. I'm on my way."

I hung up from her, and then, just in case I was about to die, I called Captain Armstrong and thanked him for helping me understand about flashbacks and for talking to me when I got scared waiting for Peavine's mom, and I apologized to him one more time for the whole MBI shoe thing and how I was stupid for a while and almost treated him like people who don't understand about war problems do. He sounded confused, but finally he said, "You're welcome, kid. Any time."

Thump.

I jumped as I hung up the phone and put it back in my pocket.

It's just Mom's mice, I tried to tell myself. *They're hungry, and—*

And I froze solid again, this time because I suddenly saw a picture that had been in my mind the whole time, hidden away, like the memories of the night of the fire. The items on my list rearranged themselves and changed, and the mystery—

No way.

But . . .

My eyes slid away from the basement door and went to the pantry. I touched my belly, which wasn't as fat as it should have been, since I'd been packing away all that food. Then I looked at the phone on the charger on the counter and thought about how Cissy and Doc's mom had called my mother.

My hands pressed into my stomach.

Couldn't be. I was 1,000 percent insane.

But . . .

But nothing. Either I had gone crazy or I hadn't. It was time to find out.

I got up, feeling a whole lot less afraid than I should have, but my hands still shook as I took two frozen meals out of the freezer. Meatloaf and mashed potatoes, my favorite. The delicious smell of gravy and meat (not fish sticks—hallelujah) seemed to fill the whole house as I cooked the meals one at a time, without letting myself think too hard about what I was doing.

What's the truth, Footer? Do you even know anymore?

No. I didn't know. Mom wouldn't tell me, and Dad couldn't tell me. So I'd just have to tell myself.

I finished cooking the meals, used some salt and pepper on the potatoes, and added a little butter. Then I dug around in the fridge until I found two containers of applesauce. I loaded the applesauce, some napkins, two drink boxes, and silverware into a grocery bag, picked up the meals, and carried them to the basement door.

When I opened it, a *clink* echoed through the house, like one of Dad's weights was being set on the floor.

I kept listening.

I thought I made out the soft *whump* of the door of the little bedroom shutting.

I carried the meatloaf meals down the steps, slow so I didn't spill anything. When I got to the little bedroom, I had to set them on the floor to turn the door handle.

The door pushed open easily.

When I looked into the room, that's when I started to get nervous.

It seemed spotless and completely empty. No sounds. No unusual smells. No movement. I picked up the meatloaf meals and went inside, glancing at the bathroom and each of the room's corners. The single closet door was shut, but when I spoke, I directed my words at the bed—under it, to be exact, because under the bed made more sense than anything.

"I know you're in here."

No response came from the bed.

"I figured you were tired of peanut butter and lunch junk, so I made you some real dinner. Well, mostly real. It's not fish sticks, at least."

Heart beating fast now, I stood there holding the meals and watching the bed and waiting. Nothing happened.

You're crazy, my brain told me. *Completely bonkers. Deranged, insane, certifiable. Out to lunch, screwy, nuts. Looney, flaky, cuckoo.* The insults went on forever. I probably could have stood there a few hours thinking up new ones, but I didn't think we had that kind of time before Steph showed up.

"You might as well come out and talk to me," I told the bed. *Half-baked, one bushel shy of a full crop, not playing with a full deck.* "I found the letters from Carl Abrams, and I think I remember most of what happened."

Mental. A fruitcake. A freak.

Out of my tree. Off my gourd. Completely unhinged.

I sighed. "Look, my DCFS worker is on the way, and the police will be here soon to talk to Dad about everything, and they'll probably search the house and find you. You want to go with them full or starving?"

Goofy. Psycho. Touched in the head.

The bedspread moved a fraction, right at the bottom. I saw a little hand, just a flash of fingers, then it was gone. I jumped hard enough that I almost dropped the meatloaf trays, but managed to keep hold of them even though hot gravy sloshed on both of my thumbs.

Somebody let out a loud breath.

Then the bedspread moved a lot, and I saw the top of a head with black hair. Then I saw the rest of a head and some shoulders. . . .

And finally a whole girl crawled out, dragging her long legs until she could crouch on the floor.

CHAPTER 18

It Doesn't Matter Anymore When the Fire Was, Does It?

Cissy Abrams stared straight at me.

I stood between her and the little bedroom door and stared right back at her. I waited for my ears to buzz and for my nose to tell me I was smelling smoke. I waited for the world to change and to see things and get dizzy and pass out and spill meatloaf everywhere.

Nothing happened, except that I felt relieved. Everything went quiet inside me, for the first time since the Abrams fire.

Nothing kept right on happening after that, except Cissy and me staring at each other, even when I squinted at her hands and arms, searching for any trace of the blood flecks from my nightmares and flashbacks. Of course there weren't any. She would have showered since then, in the bathroom attached to the little bedroom, probably while I was at school and Dad worked. Her dark hair looked clean enough, and she had it pulled back in a neon-green scrunchie I recognized as one of Mom's. She had on a pair of Mom's white shorts, too, and one of Mom's yellow tank tops. Her feet were bare, but they weren't dirty, and she had that pale look people get when they stay inside all the time or use whole bottles of sunscreen and wear big floppy sunhats and sit under umbrellas.

Cissy must have decided I wasn't going to scream or bite her, because she reached under the bed and helped her brother out from their hiding place. Doc escaped the bedspread faster and easier, then stood up before his sister did, his dark-brown eyes fixed on the meatloaf plates in my hand. His long, curly black hair hadn't been combed in a while. He wore a pair of my dad's red boxers as gigantic shorts, and one of dad's white sleeveless T-shirts, all bunched around his skinny waist like a toga. None of that struck me as funny, because mottled, fading yellows and greens made up the left side of his face. Even in the dim lighting, I could tell that his eye had gotten punched really bad and hard, though it had gotten better in the fifteen days since everything happened.

I didn't have any words, so I held out the meatloaf trays.

Doc looked at Cissy.

She nodded, and he came and took the meals from my hands, then ran back to the bed with them. Before I could hand him the grocery bag with the napkins and silverware, he started eating the food with his fingers. I didn't say anything about that. I just took everything to him, except one napkin that I used to wipe gravy off my hands. Then I backed off to stand in the bedroom door again, keeping my eyes on him and his sister. That bruise on his face, it hurt me to look at it. I bet it hurt Doc to chew, maybe even to speak, but he seemed to swallow well enough.

For a time, Cissy and I just watched Doc eat. He stabbed straws into the juice boxes, drinking both of them about as fast as he ate both dinners. When he found the silverware and napkins, he used them. That struck me as a good thing. Maybe he hadn't gone totally wild like some wolf-boy out in the forest, even though his gaze darted around the room between bites, checking on Cissy, then on me, then on the open door.

"Does he talk?" I asked her, surprised when my voice worked.

"Used to," Cissy said, her voice quiet. She had a deep accent, like folks from way down in the Delta. "Ain't spoke a word since that night. My mom's supposed to pick us up. You seen her?"

I frowned. "She called. I don't think she's coming."

Cissy gave me a quick, miserable look, then went back to studying her brother. "Shoulda known better than to count on her. Sorry about all the food we've been eating, and about your mom getting hurt with that big gun. Man, she's laid up a long time over that."

"She's in Memphis," I mumbled, "in a psychiatric hospital."

Cissy's eyes widened. "I'm real sorry about that too, then."

It took me a second, but I got hold of myself. "The food's no big deal. And Mom—" I couldn't figure what to say about that, so I borrowed Dad's words. "Mom is nobody's fault."

Cissy hung her head like she didn't quite buy that last bit. Then she raised up straight again and looked at me. Her eyes seemed a lot more alive now that I was sure I wasn't seeing a ghost or hallucination or flashback.

"We got to go," she said.

My pulse jumped all over again. "What? No. Help's coming. You stay right here."

"I'm the one did the shooting, and I set the fire, too." Cissy's voice was dead calm as she moved away from me, heading toward the basement steps. "So when the police come, they'll take me, and won't be nobody to look after my brother."

"Wait!" I turned and raised my hands too fast, and she flinched away from me. Doc dropped his fork and scrabbled backward on the bed, dumping potatoes on the spread. I held up both hands. "I'm sorry. Didn't mean to scare you. It's just—you did it, Cissy? The shooting and the fire? All of it?"

Her head bobbed once, her eyes fixed somewhere over my shoulder. "Had to. If I hadn't shot him, he woulda killed my brother."

"Yeah, I know. I saw all that. But the fire?"

"I set it to keep the old jackass busy 'cause we was trying to run off, but he caught us. I thought he'd piddle around with the blaze in the barn, and we'd be gone. Your mom was gonna help us get to our mom, simple as that." Her gaze shifted back to my face, and she looked miserable again. "At least, it was supposed to be simple."

Across the room on the bed, Doc started shoveling down the food again. The reality that I was having a conversation with Cissy Abrams edged into my awareness, along with the fact that she was about to leave and nobody in the universe would ever believe they had even been here.

Mom's innocent.

My mom hadn't done anything at all, except try to help Cissy and Doc—but if they left, how would I ever prove any of that?

"You have to stay," I said. "The police think Mom accidentally killed you, because I thought that and I put it in a list, and Peavine's little sister gave the list to his mom. But, anyway, they're all coming, the police and Steph—she's my DCFS worker—and they're going to think Mom did all that bad stuff, and this is a total mess."

I turned circles, pushing my palms into the sides of

my head to make myself think while Cissy stared at me like she figured I really was a few clowns shy of a circus. Panic turned me completely stupid, and I knew it, but I couldn't think of a better plan. I stopped turning circles, zipped out of the little bedroom, closed the door to the basement steps, grabbed hold of Dad's weight bench, and slid it across the floor to block the way out to the rest of the house. Then I planted myself between Cissy and the door to the backyard. I could still see all the way into the bedroom and keep my eyes on both her and Doc.

"I can't stay here," Cissy said again, sounding more confused than angry. "I'll go to juvenile, and Doc can't be alone."

"My friend Steph will help you." I stood very still, barely able to breathe, heart smashing against my ribs, but I was pretty sure I was telling her the truth. I hoped she didn't jump for the weight bench. What was I going to do, tackle her?

"Steph," Cissy muttered.

"My DCFS worker, yeah."

"You think some DCFS worker's gonna help me?" Cissy sounded skeptical. She put out her hand for Doc, who ignored her and kept eating.

"She has fake hair," I said, louder than I meant to. "But she's okay, once you tell her what you like and don't like."

The mower still hadn't shut off outside. I wished

it would get suddenly, totally dark. Dad would have to come in then. He'd see everything, and he'd know.

Cissy's eyes flicked to the door that led outside.

I held out my arms so she'd know I wasn't planning on letting her get past me.

"Come on, now," she said to Doc. "Get over here this second."

"Don't go," I pleaded, but Doc came to Cissy like she had told him to do, and she went straight to the weight bench and started pulling it out of the way.

Desperate, I jumped forward and grabbed the edges of the seat, but too late. Cissy shoved it aside, then opened the door to the rest of the house, and she and Doc jogged up the steps, away from me. I charged after them, intending to follow them all the way across the neighborhood if I had to, but my feet tangled before I got to the door.

I screamed as I pitched forward, hitting the stairs hard on my left shoulder and arm. Agony blazed through my wrist. I screamed again and again. The world spun as I flipped and grabbed for anything to stop myself from falling down the stairs.

I landed hard at the bottom of the steps, on my left side again. My wrist pulsed with pain, and the world tried to go black. I saw darkness and Dad's weight bench and the door Cissy and Doc had run through, to disappear forever.

Spots danced across my vision. Darkness spread, terrible and awful and trying to cover me up and eat me whole. As I tried to shake it off, hands took hold of my shoulder, and Cissy's voice said, "Easy there. You fell pretty bad."

Just then, something small and blond and shrieking launched off the steps and landed beside us. My head spun as I watched Stephanie Bridges grab hold of Cissy like she was some kind of robber or criminal. Doc tried to bolt, but she grabbed his arm too.

"Don't hurt them," I yelled, then coughed and cried out from the agony in my wrist. "You have to help them. Please."

"Footer!" Captain Armstrong's worried voice boomed down the stairs. "Kid! You there?" He charged into view, carrying a rifle bigger than me.

Sirens. I heard them now. They were close and coming closer.

Steph squeaked when she saw the rifle and waved her hands and tried to say something about children and danger.

"Get Dad," I said to Captain Armstrong. "Backyard. Mower." My wrist hurt so bad, I could barely get out the words. To Steph I said, "That's Cissy and Doc Abrams."

Steph seemed to realize who she was holding on to, and her mouth came open. She let Cissy and Doc go and covered her mouth with one hand. With the other, she took the rifle Captain Armstrong handed her.

"I knew you didn't sound right on the phone," Captain Armstrong said as he stepped over me. "I called 9-1-1 and told them to send a car right away, and an ambulance in case—"

He stopped. Cleared his throat.

"In case I was losing it, like Mom?"

Captain Armstrong frowned. "Not that, exactly. But you've been through a lot lately. I know how that can be. Help's coming, Footer."

I thought about being mad at him, but my wrist hurt too bad, and he was only being nice. And right. Some part of me knew that.

He headed for the basement door without saying anything else. Steph kept her hand over her mouth and held the rifle away from her like it would start dancing and shooting all on its own. I tried to sit up as Cissy Abrams knelt and helped me get upright, then shook her head at the black and purple wrist I cradled against my chest.

"That's broke, Footer," she said.

"I know." Tears leaked out of my eyes. I didn't know if I was crying because my wrist hurt or because I was alive or because Cissy and Doc were alive or because I was pretty sure I wasn't crazy or because Mom wouldn't get in trouble for all my mistakes.

"That woman's gonna pass out if somebody don't take

that rifle away from her," Cissy said as she got up again.

"I know," I repeated. Talking hurt.

Cissy inched toward Steph, who didn't so much as twitch or take a breath. I heard men talking, but I didn't hear Dad yet. "I want my father," I whispered, but nobody heard me. I cried harder, and that hurt too.

Flashlights danced across the walls. A lot of people in uniforms came running into the basement, from out back and from down the stairs.

"It's okay, ma'am," Cissy said as she gently removed the rifle from Steph's immobile fingers. "You won't be needin' to use this."

When she handed the rifle to the police officer nearest her, an older lady I didn't know, the lady must have recognized Cissy. I heard her whistle, then say, "Well, I'll swanee. You're one of those missing kids."

An EMS worker dropped to his knees beside me and held out his hand to examine my wrist. When I moved my hurt arm, that nasty blackness finally caught up to me.

"Dad," I whispered again, but he still wasn't there. All the sounds and lights faded to nothing. As my eyes closed, I couldn't stop wanting to see him, and I couldn't do anything to stop the darkness.

CHAPTER 19

Dark . . .

Dad?

Dark . . .

Dad!

My stomach clenched and my eyes came open, and I squinted at the blazing white light. White walls. White sheets. Machines. Everything smelled like alcohol.

Hospital!

I sat up, pulling tubes with me, then coughed and cried because moving hurt my wrist so much. It had some kind of stiff brace on it. I grabbed at the Velcro straps.

"Easy there, Miss Davis." A nurse moved my uninjured wrist back to my side and patted my hand, which had a butterfly-shaped needle in it, covered by tape. The needle was hooked to a tube that went to a bag next to a machine with numbers on it.

"This is an IV," the nurse explained. She was tiny and blond and looked a lot like Steph. "We use these to give you fluids and medicine if you need it. And this"—she gently touched the fiberglass brace—"you need a cast on that wrist, so we have to keep it immobilized until it's set. That way we won't have to take you to surgery to do it."

Surgery? No way. I stopped moving my hurt arm and my good arm too. My hurt arm could lie there until the cast people showed up, or however that worked. No problem.

"I want my dad." My voice sounded crackly like school speakers when I talked, but I sounded like I really meant it, and I think I did.

"Okay. I'll tell him you're awake."

Dad was here somewhere.

My muscles went weak, and my head sagged, and I breathed in and out, in and out, listening to the sound and knowing that Dad was nearby and he'd come and sit with me.

The nurse slipped out of the cubicle, letting the sheet-like curtains sway behind her. After she left, I let myself really look around. White everywhere, except the silver tray near the end of the bed. It had weird-looking scissors on it, and white tape like the tape holding my IV.

My heart started beating funny, a little too hard and a little too fast. It didn't feel good. Mom hated hospitals. I hadn't had to be in one before as a patient, but I thought she had a point. It seemed weird. I sort of felt tied down, with the IV and the wrist immobilizer, and also because the bed was kind of high. I'd probably break something else if I tried to get down.

Were Cissy and Doc here too? I looked around a little more, but I didn't see any shadows moving around outside the sheet-walls. Did they run away? Did enough people see them to know they were alive and Mom didn't kill them?

I closed my eyes and tried to think about that YouTube video I watched on calming down. It didn't help much, but I breathed as relaxingly as I could, letting my stomach move up and down with each inhale and exhale.

"Footer." Dad's voice rumbled through the tiny curtained space, sounding relieved and worried at the same time. "How's my girl?"

My eyes popped open.

Dad grinned at me, sort of real and sort of fake, like he was trying really hard to make me feel okay. I didn't say anything, because if I tried to talk, I'd cry, and that would tick me off, and all of a sudden I was ticked off anyway, and I didn't even know why.

Dad gazed at me like he was waiting for me to say something.

All that came to me was, "Cissy and Doc?"

"They're here," Dad said. "The doctors are checking them out, and Stephanie Bridges is with them. Cissy won't let go of her. She says you told her Steph would help her, so she doesn't want to talk to any other DCFS worker."

I nodded.

"Honey, how are you?"

Leave me alone. It almost came out, but it didn't. What was wrong with me? Was this some kind of new crazy coming after me now, when I thought everything was finally okay?

No. I'm not crazy. Not yet, anyway.

Dad kept looking at me with that weird grin on his face. "How long did you know those kids were in our basement?"

I thought about my puzzle list, the one I sent Peavine. I had been right about most of them things on it, but about Mom setting the fire and Cissy and Doc being dead I had been so wrong, and I was glad. "I didn't figure it out until tonight, but I should have known sooner."

Dad's eyebrows came together. "Why?"

"All the food disappearing. I thought I was eating it in my sleep, but I just should have known I couldn't pack away *that* much."

Dad kept his eyebrows still this time, but his jaw worked, and I could tell he was surprised and maybe confused. "You thought you were sleepwalking and sleep-eating? Why didn't you tell me?"

"Why would I?" My voice came out loud enough to make me twitch, so I clamped my teeth together. "You didn't even notice all the food getting disappeared."

Dad would probably get mad now and lecture me for hollering at him, and ground me. Whatever. I was too mad to care, and I still didn't know why.

"Footer—"

"You think I'm sick, don't you?" I yelled again, but I couldn't help it. "Sick like Mom. You think it's happening to me."

Dad raised both hands. "I—no. That's not it."

"You're lying. You think I'm crazy, and that's why you didn't believe me when I tried to tell you about Mom and the fire and everything."

Dad's hands came down, and he gaped at me. A bunch of emotions moved across his face. I saw more surprise and a little bit of mad, then sadness. Each feeling seemed a thousand times bigger because it was Dad and not Mom, and Dad didn't usually show that much emotion.

"That's . . . not it," he said again, in a quiet voice, almost weak sounding, and I didn't believe him, and I don't think he even believed himself.

"I'm in the hospital like Mom was before she got sent to Memphis." Not yelling. Better. But not by much. "Are you going to have me sent to some unit like that somewhere, for kids?"

"What? No. Why would you think that?"

"The way you're looking at me right now!" Anger rushed through me, so hot it doubled the sweat running down the back of my neck. "You didn't believe me when I tried to talk to you, and I'm mad about it and I'm yelling, so you think I'm going crazy and you have to be all careful with me."

"No." And now Dad's face showed more misery than I had ever seen before in my life, so much that it smushed my anger to nothing and made my heart hurt almost as much as my broken wrist.

"I don't get to be mad at Mom because she lied to me and didn't tell me stuff and almost blew up our lives," I said, more to the covers than to Dad. "Being mad at her doesn't help anything, and she won't even remember half of this mess when she's better. I don't have her, sometimes. I don't have her a *lot* of the time. What am I going to do if I don't have you, either?"

Dad sat on the edge of my bed, on the side with my bad arm. He did it slow and easy so he wouldn't hurt me. I stared into his face and saw lines around his eyes and his mouth, and he looked older than I remembered. My heart hurt a little worse. Dad had always seemed like Captain Armstrong—big and powerful and indestructible. Right now he seemed as breakable as Mom and me.

He kept his gaze on the floor for a time, and I let him, even though I didn't feel mad anymore and I just wanted to cry and hear him make stupid jokes again, and this time try to make jokes back so he wouldn't be sad anymore.

"You're right," he said in a voice so quiet, I had to lean forward to hear him. "Sometimes I don't notice things I should. I think I do that because I'm scared, Footer, and I'm sorry."

That made my mouth come open. My father was a

soldier and a policeman. He wasn't afraid of anything. He was like my anti-scaredy-cat Superman. "What are you scared of?" I asked him, not even having to try to sound nice now.

Dad kept right on staring at the floor, and I saw his shoulders shake when he breathed. He stayed quiet so long I thought maybe he wasn't going to tell me, but then he said, "I'm afraid of losing your mother, just like you are. I'm afraid of losing you—my family, everything I love."

Before I could say anything, he raised his head and looked at me. "I want to promise you something. You'll never lose me, Footer. No matter what, I'll always be right here. Give me another chance, and I'll do better about listening to you and believing you—and believing *in* you."

I kept staring at him.

He really looked like he meant it. Then tears rolled down both of his cheeks, and the hurt in my heart made me cry too.

Once the tears started, I couldn't stop them, and I couldn't stop my mouth, either. "Will I ever get to stop worrying about losing my mind? Because sometimes I worry about it a whole lot, and when you worry about it too I can't stand it. I get so scared. I'm tired of being scared."

"Me too." He faced me and lifted one hand to stroke my cheek and brush away my tears. "For what it's worth, I don't think you're sick like your mother. I think you're perfect and smart and pretty and strong, and nothing else matters. Whatever comes down the road later, we'll deal with it—but for now I think our biggest problem is that busted purple wrist of yours."

The agony in my chest eased, and my tears slowed. My busted purple wrist kept right on hurting, though. I moved it just enough to get Dad to look at it. "I don't know about this wrist being our biggest issue. Have you seen your face lately? Do they make wrinkle cream for guys?"

"I don't think it's called wrinkle cream, but yeah." Dad's grin made everything hurt a little bit less.

"Good, 'cause you look way older than you should."

"That's cold, Footer."

I managed a grin of my own. "Truth is hard, Dad."

"Keep it up," he said, wiping away the last of my tears. "One more crack and I'll feed you walrus sticks for breakfast when we finally get home."

The face I made must have been epic, because Dad was still smiling about it when the nurse came to take me to the cast room.

From the Notebook of Kay Malone
Because Peavine Let Me Read His Detective Notebook and Angel Let Me Read Her Astronaut Notebook and Doing Interviews Looked Like So Much Fun, Even If I'm Talking to Myself. Hey, It's Safer Than Hunting Walruses.

Already Lonely Teacher: How I will miss you next year, Footer Davis. Fifth grade won't be the same without you. You are braver than five people put together. At least you made it back before the year ended, so you'll get to come to all the cupcake parties. That makes me happier than all the reporters skulking around. Are you rethinking this journalism thing yet? You did pretty great on the detective part, you know.
Happy Teacher: I'm glad I got to sign your bright-yellow wrist cast before everybody else did!
Grateful Teacher: I'm very glad your mom may get to come home next week. The police were right not to charge her with anything when she was just trying to help two abused children. Stephanie Bridges was a plague to you, but she seems to be doing okay by Cissy and Doc, driving them down to Pearl every week to see their dad, getting me to tutor them on all the lessons they missed during

the homeschooling that didn't happen, taking them to counseling, and she got them a foster home right here in town. There might be hope for that girl as she grows into her job.

Totally Nosy Teacher: Now, if I could just get you talking to Peavine again, the world might start turning like it's supposed to. Some things take time to heal, I suppose. But come on, Footer. It's been long enough.

Critical Thinking: Rewrite of My Last Paper

Footer Davis

5th Period

Ms. Perry

I am rewriting this paper because Ms. Malone and Stephanie Bridges said I shouldn't write about serial killers just to upset you. They said I could make my point better by being thorough and forthright, whatever "forthright" means. They also said I was being impolite and sort of mean. I guess they are right, so I'm sorry. Just because you are mean to me and my mother doesn't make it okay for me to be mean to you. Here is a real critical-thinking paper. I hope.

I. Hypothesis

People who are mentally ill are violent and should only live in institutions. Is this always true, sometimes true, partly true, or false?

II. Evidence Collected

Only 4 percent of violent crimes are committed by people with mental illness, like my mom. That means 96 out of 100 violent crimes are committed by completely normal people like you, but everyone thinks my mom is the scary one. My mom isn't scary. When she's sick, her thoughts move so fast, she can't even concentrate enough to think or move or make any sense. She can't plan anything. She doesn't even remember to eat if somebody doesn't help her.

My neighbor Captain Armstrong is right. Television and the movies don't really tell the truth about stuff like war and death and sickness. On television and in the movies, all the mentally ill patients slaughter people. If there's a crime show and somebody has a disorder, you can bet that person will turn out to be guilty. That's why I don't watch crime shows anymore. They just make me sad. I do read about serial killers, though, because they are truly scary, and I want to know if I run into one, so I can get away fast.

Walruses scare me too. Walruses weigh 4,000 pounds, and they have big tusks.

They can kill polar bears. It is reasonable to be afraid of walruses (and clowns, but that should be another paper). Walruses are a lot more dangerous than people like my mom, but I bet you never see a crime show where a walrus did it.

III. What I Learned from This Report

1. The hypothesis that people who have mental illness are violent and should live only in institutions is false.
2. Nobody should believe television, movies, or stuff people put on the Internet about war or death or sickness. None of that shows life or mental illness or serial killers or even walruses like they really are.
3. My mother belongs home with us, whenever she is able to be there.

B+.
You make some very good points. I hope you will take all of your future assignments this seriously.
Maybe we can both try harder not to be mean to each other.

CHAPTER 20

Three Weeks Later

"I can't believe you invited Peavine." I steadied the starter slingshot's wooden frame with my left hand. I could grip with the cast, which would probably come off next week, so I used my good hand to pull the pouch back slowly, slowly, just like Dad had been teaching me to do.

Dad watched as I let go.

The slingshot bands snapped, and the stale pink mini-marshmallow shot forward. It hit the target Dad had taped to the outside of the basement door with a soft thwack, then tumbled to the ground, leaving a tiny pink smudge on the paper. It was inside the second circle, but nowhere near the center.

"Better," Mom said from the table, underneath the big green umbrella. She turned a page in her *Newsweek* magazine. I didn't think there was an article about me or Cissy and Doc in that issue. Stuff seemed to be dying down a little, so we could live without reporters popping out of bushes and trash cans to get a comment.

"Honey, it's time to give this thing with the Joneses a rest," Dad said. "Regina Jones has always been wonderful to you. And Peavine and Angel didn't do anything wrong."

I fished a stale green marshmallow out of the bag. "Says you."

"Some secrets shouldn't be secrets, Footer." That was Mom.

I sighed.

Mom had been home for almost two weeks now and taking her medicine. Her hands trembled as she held the magazine, but only a little bit. Her mind seemed to be hers again, so of course the first thing she did was start running my life. I had been to two therapy appointments to talk about "what happened the night of the fire," and I hated them completely, but Mom said I'd be going back *until*. As in, *until* she said otherwise.

"I'm not talking to Peavine," I grumbled as I fired the green marshmallow and missed the door completely.

Dad shrugged and headed back to the grill, opening the lid and letting out the delicious scent of hamburgers and brats. "Then it's going to be a long afternoon."

A few minutes later, Captain Armstrong showed up dressed in green fatigue pants, a green T-shirt, and an Alabama ball cap to aggravate Dad and me. He brought his famous baked beans, the best ever, steeped in brown sugar and heaped with bacon. When Steph came with Cissy and Doc, they had chips and soft drinks, even though Steph didn't approve of too much junk food, strictly speaking.

"Excellent!" Steph chirped when she saw the slingshot and marshmallows. "See? I knew you could find something safe to do with your father."

Dad kept his back to her and continued messing around with the meat on the grill. Mom hardly paused in her chattering at Captain Armstrong. I chose a pink marshmallow and loaded it up as Cissy came to stand with me. She watched me shoot the edge of the target. Then she took the slingshot and fired a green marshmallow dead center into the red dot.

Steph clapped, then turned her attention to the Jones family, who were coming around the far side of the house carrying dishes covered with aluminum foil.

I looked away before I could pay too much attention to Peavine, then got seriously annoyed when I realized my heart had started to beat faster.

Cissy looked like a new person in her jeans and yellow sun top. She had her hair back off her neck, tied with a yellow bow. She handed me back my slingshot, then said in a low voice, "I'm figurin' Steph doesn't know these come in sniper versions with thirty-five-pound pulls and forty-four-caliber ammo that can kill deer?"

"Ssshh." I shot another pink marshmallow and missed

the back door totally. The marshmallow bounced on the ground and hit Doc's white sneaker. He was standing with Angel, looking at one of her megabooks. He actually had it open, like he might be reading the pages.

"Is Doc talking yet?" I asked Cissy.

"Some. I think it's going to be a while. He already met Angel in summer school, and I think she's helping."

I sighed. A conspiracy. That's what this was. I shot a green mini-marshmallow at the target and managed to hit inside the second circle.

"Not bad," Peavine said from over my left shoulder. "Think you could get good enough to kill a snake?"

My cheeks burned. I tried to look at Cissy instead of acknowledging Peavine, but Cissy walked off fast, like she had it planned all along. There was just enough of a breeze for me to catch the scent of his favorite barbecue potato chips. He probably ate them for breakfast.

My stupid heart beat even faster . . . and then I just didn't want to be mad at my best friend anymore. I closed my eyes and imagined myself looking all red-faced and ticked off. Pretty stupid. Maybe Dad was right. Maybe I should give it all a rest.

"I could probably kill a snake," I said, "but I don't think I could kill a walrus."

Peavine came up beside me then, planting his right pole close to my foot. "What about a creep eating hot dogs and wearing plaid?"

I shook my head. "I'll leave that to Dad and his friends at work." Would my hair look better pulled back like Cissy's? Jeez, I should at least comb it now and then. When I glanced over at Cissy, she was sitting next to Mom. They were both reading *Newsweek*.

Peavine held out his hand for the slingshot. I passed it to him and whispered, "Don't tell Steph you can use this to fire stuff other than marshmallows, okay?"

"Okay." He held on to my hand, our fingers closed around the slingshot's frame, the bands dangling down and bouncing against our wrists.

When I looked into Peavine's blue eyes, they were wide and sweet and sad. "I'm sorry I let Angel get hold of your note, Footer." His voice came out low, just for me to hear, and I could almost count all the tears he had cried, and all the tears I had cried. "I'm sorry I didn't try to talk Mom out of giving it to your dad. It's just—I was so worried about you. I really thought it was the best thing."

"I'm sorry I ignored your texts and calls and e-mails," I said. He nodded and let go of my hand to take the slingshot. My fingers tingled where he had touched me, and emotions I couldn't name choked me up and made me add, "Peavine, maybe you shouldn't keep trying to be my friend. Even though I'm not sick now, you know I'll probably wind up like Mom."

He picked out a green marshmallow, propped his elbows on the arm grips of his poles, and fired. The marshmallow bounced off a basement window. "If you get sick, you'll see the doctor and get medicine, and I'll still be your friend and so will Angel."

Friend. Yeah. That's what Peavine was. My best friend. He always had been. That's what he should be. The unnamed emotions swirled faster and harder, and then I felt disappointed, which made no sense at all.

He handed the slingshot back to me and grinned. "Want to go for a walk later?"

"Sure, we could pop tar bubbles. It's hot enough."

"I was thinking more like the path in the woods, only west, not south, away from the Abrams farm."

"Okay." I was about to ask him if he wanted to pick up horse apples to put in the road for cars to hit so their tires would stink, but I realized he was pulling something out of his pocket.

A box, wrapped in purple paper, with a tiny golden bow on top.

He held it out to me, his expression shifting to nervous and worried.

I dropped the slingshot onto the marshmallow bag and took the box. It was months to my birthday. Why was he giving me a present now?

He looked too nervous for me to ask him, so I slid my finger into the paper and unwrapped the box. When I pulled off the lid, I found a leather bracelet inside. Its center held a pretty brass flower, painted white with soft pink tips on the petals, just like clover. On either side of the brass clover flower, one of the bracelet's leather strands had been strung with shimmering green rocks.

"Those are aventurines," Peavine said when I touched one smooth stone. "They're for courage and luck. You got a lot of the first, but I figured you could use some of the second."

"Yeah, I could," I whispered, letting the box drop on top of the slingshot and marshmallows and holding on to the bracelet. The soft leather must have been worked a long time before it got turned into jewelry. When I touched the flower petals, they were still cool from being in the box. I fastened the bracelet around my right wrist, since it wouldn't fit over my cast. As soon as it settled into place, my fingers went straight back to the aventurines.

"They're green like your eyes." Peavine sounded less nervous. "That's why I picked them."

I looked at him to see if he was kidding.

He wasn't.

He seemed to be waiting for me to understand something, but I just kept touching the aventurines. Their smooth perfection made my worries feel small and distant and fading, like birds flying toward the sun.

Peavine pointed to the brass clover, then one of the aventurines. "Flower and rock, see? It's the answer to that question you asked me, out on the playground that day when—you know."

That day when I kissed him. Yeah, I knew. I stared at him, right at his face. He was standing so close to me that I could have counted his freckles. How many freckles did I have? Had Peavine ever wanted to count my freckles?

My face got hot all over again, and not because I was trying to be mad.

"You asked me if I thought you were more like a flower or a rock."

"Okay." I kept my fingers on the bracelet, but my gaze stayed firmly on his face. Had his eyes always been this blue, or did the sun make them brighter?

"Flowers are soft and pretty and bloom over and over again. Rocks are pretty too, but stronger, and they last longer." Peavine's grin came so naturally that I had to smile back at him. "I got that bracelet for you because you're both to me, Footer. You're a flower, but you're a rock, too."

If I kissed him after lunch, he would probably taste like hot dogs, or maybe the sweet brown sugar and bacon from Captain Armstrong's baked beans.

That would be okay by me.

"A walk would be real nice later," I said to Peavine.

He kept grinning, and so did I.

Then we went to eat lunch with Mom and Dad and Ms. Jones and Steph and Captain Armstrong and Cissy and Doc, and no copperheads, no walruses, and no serial killers. I thought about taking pictures on my phone like a good journalist, but sometimes pictures don't say everything, and besides, I didn't want to be a journalist anymore.

Maybe I could make jewelry like my beautiful bracelet, or be in the army like Dad and Captain Armstrong and join a police department when I got out, or make bright, colored casts like the orthopedist who fixed up my wrist. There was always dancing, too. Maybe I shouldn't have given up so easily on being a ballerina or a poet or an artist. Social worker recently made the list too, thanks to Steph—or maybe I could just win some lottery money like Ms. Jones. After all, I had luck now, right?

I'm a flower and a rock, I thought as I passed Peavine a plate full of hot dogs and a big, giant helping of baked beans. I held up my bracelet, loving how the green stones winked and glittered in the sun. *I'm a flower and a rock, and later I'll take a walk with my best friend.*

That seemed like a pretty great afternoon to me.

Acknowledgments

Writing middle-grade fiction was a new venture for me, and so many people deserve thanks and recognition.

Of course my family gets a nod, for putting up with my writing process, and listening endlessly to all the chapters. Gisele, JB, and Gynni, you are great. Karen, thank you, too, for sitting through all the readings and never beating your head against a wall.

A big, sparkly bow to Stelmo, for reading. Thanks to Judy and Julie and Shannon and Jennifer for encouraging me with my writing. Blushing appreciation to Charlotte and Mom and Lindy and Valerie for being proud to show people my books. Massive hugs to Rondell and Tina for giving me social-work advice and opinions, and special kudos to Chris, who answers every technical and mechanical question I come up with—and without ever laughing at me! Thank you, Jim, for keeping my spirits up during a dark time.

For my wonderful agent, Erin—what can I say? You knew I wanted to do this, and you knew I could, and you held my hand. Thank you so much for searching with me until we found the right thing for me and for my writing. Sharyn, thank you for breaking the Facebook wall and giving me encouragement, too. One day when the time and the story are right . . .

And now for Sylvie, my editor. I'm so happy to be working with you! I can't express enough gratitude to you for taking the chance, fighting for my book, finding a title I didn't hate, and being SO EASY to work with, on little things and big things and everything in between. I love your style and your feel for character and voice, and your willingness to teach me in this area I know so little about. Thank you also for the cool mailer, for using the actual U.S. Mail to reach me in rural Kentucky, and for thinking my giant dog is adorable. And big. Yes, he's big. I promise to find someplace the monster can't reach, so I never have to actually call you and tell you the dog ate my edits (hey, it was a near miss).

Author's Note

From the Notebook of Sylvie Frank, Editor (Cause Ms. Malone is right, interview notebooks are totally fun)

Interview of Susan Vaught, Author (who really did want to be a detective and an astronaut and a dancer and a painter, but turned into a psychologist and a writer instead)

Location: In her living room, in her cabin in the woods, on the telephone next to her parrot's cage (hello, noisy parrot!)

Editor: Let's start with a hard one. Why'd you write this book?

S. V.: Because walruses are creepy.
Okay, okay. I wrote this book for the same reason I write all my books—characters start talking in my head, and I really want to give them a story. Footer didn't just talk in my head, she drew, so that made this extra-special fun as I worked on it. The sketch of the doodlebug started it all, and Footer's opinion that whoever named her town after lice was not right in the head.

Editor: Is any of this story based on real life?

S. V.: When I was eight years old, in Corinth, Mississippi, my mother actually did shoot a snake off our back pond using my stepfather's elephant gun. It sounded like enemy aircraft had dropped a bomb in the yard. The windows shook, leaves fell—and Mom knocked herself backward up several steps and badly bruised her shoulder. None of us could hear right for a week. Neighbors came to check to see what on earth had happened, and everybody got a huge laugh out of it. The snake was dead. Really, really dead. Have to give her that much!

Editor: Footer's mom has bipolar disorder, and Footer worries that she might also have it. First of all, what is bipolar disorder? And second, is her fear justified?

S. V.: To answer your first question, the National Institute of Mental Health defines it as "a brain disorder that causes unusual shifts in mood, energy, activity levels, and the ability to carry out day-to-day tasks. Symptoms of bipolar disorder are severe. They are different from the normal ups and downs that everyone goes through from time to time. Bipolar disorder symptoms can result in damaged relationships, poor job or school performance, and even suicide. But bipolar disorder can be treated, and people with this illness can lead full and productive lives." Translation: big ups and downs in mood that can cause a lot of trouble for people experiencing them, and their friends and family. And to answer your second question, 5.5 to 6 million people in the United States are diagnosed with this disorder, which comes to 2.5 to 3 percent of the adult population. It does often run in families. If a parent has bipolar disorder, there is a higher risk that the children will have it—about one out of every ten children with a parent who has bipolar disorder will also have it (around 10 percent). If both parents have it, then the odds jump to 30 percent. So sure, Footer is within bounds to worry. She has a 10 percent chance of getting the disorder—but she has a 90 percent chance that she won't. The odds are in her favor.

Editor: When will Footer know if she's going to have bipolar disorder?

S. V.: That's a harder question to answer. Most people develop symptoms that doctors recognize around age twenty-five. Some people do get symptoms earlier, even in childhood. Others get symptoms later. It's an uncertainty Footer's going to have to live with for a while.

Editor: If Footer gets bipolar disorder, is everything going to be horrible for her?

S. V.: No, but having bipolar disorder isn't easy. She would face more challenges, but with education and medication, bipolar disorder can be managed just like other medical illness, like diabetes or hypertension.

Unfortunately, many societies, including our own, are still not accepting or understanding of brain disorders. In the United States we have tended to think like Footer's teacher Ms. Perry and literally lock away groups of people who are different from other people. Until the 1980s, if somebody was born with intellectual impairment or brain impairment, they were placed in institutions, never given any choices or options in their own lives, and never allowed to be out in society for people to begin to learn about their challenges or strengths and to see how much they can contribute to our world.

Editor: Is this changing?

S. V.: Yes! The United States is beginning to join with other countries in adopting the Recovery Model, which is more about building supports to make sure that anyone with a brain disorder can get the treatment he or she needs, help people understand and cope with these disorders, and help people make choices and become productive in their own lives. It is also about getting rid of all the unnecessary challenges people face due to society's attitudes, lack of knowledge, and fears and prejudice.

Editor: How do you know all this stuff?

S. V.: I have two jobs! Being a writer is one of those. Most days, though, I work at my other job as a clinical neuropsychologist. I have a doctoral degree in clinical psychology and intellectual disability research, and I specialize in helping people who have severe brain disorders due to genetics, injury, or severe mental illness. So I keep up with all the latest research and information. You don't have to go to school to be a doctor to learn a lot of what I know, though. You can look at the links I put together, right after this note.

Editor: Okay, okay, but now the REALLY important questions. Does Footer have bipolar disorder? Does her mom keep getting better? Does she marry Peavine and get to be a journalist?

S. V.: Well . . . if Footer *does* have bipolar disorder, she'll still have an amazing life because it's manageable and she's an amazing person. If Footer's mom can keep working with her doctors and find treatment that works for her and that she can adhere to, she'll be able to be the mom Footer believes she needs. As for Footer and Peavine, well, I'm definitely rooting for them.

Further Reading

Books and E-Books

Nonfiction

Covey, Stephen R. *The Seven Habits of Highly Effective People.* New York: Free Press, 1989.

Grass, Gayle. *He Shoots! He Scores!* Perth, ON: Iris the Dragon, 2010.

SANE Australia. *You're Not Alone: A SANE Guide to Mental Illness for Children.* Australia: SANE Australia, 2003.

Fiction

Gantos, Jack. *Joey Pigza Swallowed the Key.* New York: Macmillan, 1998.

Sones, Sonya. *Stop Pretending: What Happened When My Big Sister Went Crazy.* New York: HarperTeen, 1999.

Trueman, Terry. *Inside Out.* New York: HarperTeen, 2004.

Vaught, Susan. *Freaks Like Us.* New York: Bloomsbury, 2012.

Websites

CAMH
www.camh.ca/
Canada's Centre for Addiction and Mental Health offers a guide just for kids who have parents with bipolar disorder, answering a lot of common questions.

Iris the Dragon
www.iristhedragon.com
Iris the Dragon offers a number of free e-books on mental health issues, designed for younger people.

Mental Health Reporting
depts.washington.edu/mhreport/facts_violence.php
The University of Washington's social work department has a wonderful mental health reporting website, to help people who are learning about mental health and disorders sort out fact from myths. They do it "by the numbers," summarizing actual research results.

NIMH

www.nimh.nih.gov

The mission of the National Institute of Mental Health, "Envisions a world in which mental illnesses are prevented and cured." This site has a lot of free information booklets about disorders and also discusses all the research being done to cure them in the United States and worldwide. Parts of the website are pretty technical and heavily science oriented.

SAMHSA

http://www.samhsa.gov

In their own words, "The Substance Abuse and Mental Health Services Administration (SAMHSA) is the agency within the U.S. Department of Health and Human Services that leads public health efforts to advance the behavioral health of the nation. SAMHSA's mission is to reduce the impact of substance abuse and mental illness on America's communities." The website is packed full of information about recovery and resources, and they have a great newsletter.

SANE

www.sane.org/sane-media

SANE Australia has a lot of good guides about mental illness, written for people of all ages. You can read about mental illness overall, or about each specific disorder. You can read guides for people who have family members or friends experiencing problems, or guides for you, if you have a brain disorder.